I0742849

THE TWIN FLAMES

A DIVINE MASCULINE/ DIVINE FEMININE UNION OR IS IT?

ROSE WATSON-RICHARDSON

ISBN: 978-1-957956-33-6 (SC)
ISBN: 978-1-957956-34-3 (E)

Rev. date: 08/31/2022

DEDICATION

THIS BOOK IS DEDICATED TO ALL OF THE JOHNNIE HARRIS' AND RICO ROBINS IN SMALL TOWN USA EVERYWHERE.

THANK YOU BOTH FOR ALLOWING ME TO WEAVE A FANTASY FOR MY READERS TO ENJOY INVOLVING YOU.

FOR THE WONDERFUL AND DEAR PEOPLE OF MAHOGANY VALLEY, OHIO THANK YOU FOR ALL OF THE SUPPORT AND LOVE IT IS TRULY APPRECIATED.

FOR MY FAMILY AND FRIENDS WHO CONTINUE TO GIVE UNCONDITION LOVE AND SUPPORT, THANK YOU.

TO THE FOLKS AT LEAVITT PEAK PRESS PUBLISHING THANK YOU FOR

ALL THE DEDICATION, TIME, EFFORT TO MAKE THIS BOOK A SUCCESS.

AND LAST BUT NEVER LEAST, TO MY FOREVER LOVE, MY SOUL MATE, SOUL TIE, AND TRUE TWIN FLAME, LET'S CONTINUE BUILDING OUR EMPIRE TOGETHER FOR YOU ARE MOST TRULY MY DIVINE MASCULINE AND I AM YOUR ONE AND ONLY DIVINE FEMININE.

SIGNED,

THE EMPRESS

AS ABOVE SO BELOW

AS WITHOUT SO WITHIN

CHAPTER 1

THE BEGINNING

It was during late June or early July when her sister informed her that they would be attending a birthday bash that was being thrown by childhood friends who were siblings. The event was held at a popular place in the city where several events were held yearly, and the location was very convenient for all its attendees.

She politely informed her sister Shia that she had already promised to attend two other events on the very same night,

BUT HER SISTER WAS NOT HAVING IT, AND WOULD NOT EXCEPT NO FOR AN ANSWER. SO, SHE PULLED OUT ONE OF HER FAVORITE RED DRESSES THAT HAD BEEN HANGING IN HER CLOSET WITH TAGS STILL ATTACHED JUST WAITING FOR A NIGHT LIKE THIS. SOMEHOW, SHE COULD FEEL IN HER SPIRIT THAT THIS NIGHT WOULD BE MAGICAL. AND SO, IT WAS.

CHAPTER 2

THE MAGIC BEGINS

Rhea Richards first attended a party of a beautiful female friend of her late mother and a church vocalist whom she had known since childhood whom she adored. She sang happy birthday, posed for a few photos with various friends, then made her way to her car in route of her next event.

As she entered the next event, she was greeted by a nice young man who appeared to be in his late pre-teens who politely took her arm and escorted her to the main event hall.

THE BIRTHDAY BASH WAS ONE OF THE MOST ELEGANT, WELL-COORDINATED, AND JUST PLAIN AWESOME PARTIES SHE'D BEEN TO SINCE HER DAYS ON THE WEST COAST AND SHE WAS VERY IMPRESSED. AFTER SAYING HELLO TO THE BEAUTIFUL AND EXCEPTIONALLY TALENTED HOSTESS, SHE SPOTTED HER SIBLING WHO WAS EQUALLY AS TALENTED AS AN ENTERTAINER AND SINGER WHO WAVED FROM ACROSS THE ROOM.

IT WAS FUNNY HOW SOME THIRTY PLUS YEARS LATER SHE COULD STILL REMEMBER HIM IN SOME OF THE VARIETY SHOWS HE HAD WON PERFORMING WITH HIS GROUP OR SIBLINGS BACK THEN. THE WHOLE FAMILY WAS TALENTED IT SEEMED, AND SHE WAS DELIGHTED THAT SHE HAD COME TO ENJOY THEIR PERFORMANCES WHICH BROUGHT UP FEELINGS OF NOSTALGIA FROM CHILDHOOD.

RICO ROBINS STILL HAD A STRONG, MELODIOUS AND SOULFUL VOICE

THAT CARRIED A WIDE RANGE WHICH ALLOWED HIM TO PERFORM SONGS BY SUCH GREATS AS SAM COOKE AS WELL AS A VARIETY OF OTHER ARTISTS. RHEA KNEW THAT HE HAD PORTRAYED SEVERAL ARTISTS IN VARIOUS PLACES AND PERFORMANCES ALL OVER THE COUNTRY AND ABROAD THAT ADDED TO HIS PROFESSIONAL PORTFOLIO.

SHE APPROACHED HIM SLOWLY AND CAUTIOUSLY AS SHE HAD ALWAYS DONE EVEN AS A YOUNG GIRL. ONLY THIS TIME, SOMETHING SEEMED DIFFERENT BETWEEN THEM. SOMETHING THAT SHE COULD NOT QUITE UNDERSTAND. A FEELING, HIS AURA, HIS TOUCH ALL SEEMED TO START A FIRE IN HER BELLY THAT TRAVELED UPWARDS TO HER BREASTS AND DOWN BETWEEN HER THIGHS. A FLAME THAT WAS LIT BETWEEN THEM THAT NIGHT WHICH NEITHER OF THEM HAD SEEN COMING. NOR COULD EITHER HAVE EVER PREDICTED THAT THEY WERE IN FACT PREDESTINED TO BE IN EACH OTHER'S LIFE BY DIVINE

APPOINTMENT FROM THE ALMIGHTY HIMSELF!

THEN SUDDENLY, HE KISSED HER. THE HORMONES IN HER BODY WERE SCREAMING SO LOUD THAT SHE ALMOST MISSED HIS GENTLE WHISPER SAYING HE HAD BEEN WAITING TO SEE HER TONIGHT. SHE ALMOST WALKED AWAY WITHOUT SPEAKING OR RESPONDING WHEN SHE SUDDENLY HEARD HERSELF SAYING HAPPY BIRTHDAY, EVERYTHING IS QUITE LOVELY, THANK YOU FOR THE INVITE.

THEY BRIEFLY DISCUSSED TAKING A BIRTHDAY PIC TOGETHER AND AS SHE TURNED TO LEAVE, HE STOPPED HER AND PLANTED ANOTHER KISS ON HER CHERRY RED LIPS WHICH IGNITED THE FLAME IN HER BODY ALL OVER AGAIN. THIS IS CRAZY, SHE THOUGHT, I'M ACTING LIKE A TEEN AGE GIRL WITH RAGING HORMONES INSTEAD OF A MIDDLE-AGED WOMAN. RHEA IMMEDIATELY WENT TO DRINK TWO ICE COLD BOTTLES OF SPRING WATER AND WILLED HER BODY TO COOL DOWN.

"I saw you over there talking to Rico", her sister Shia said. Why are you so thirsty and breathing so heavy? "Just a hot flash Rhea lied, I 'll step outside and get some air in a moment." She had no way of explaining what had just taken place to anyone because she did not understand any of this herself. She excused herself and dashed off to the lady's room before leaving the event. She knew this had always been her M.O. When things get too hot to handle, run. And things had most certainly gotten hot to the 10th power just now.

CHAPTER 3

THE BOULEVARD CAFE

RHEA HEADED SOUTH TO HER NEXT EVENT, UNAWARE THAT HER EX-FIANCÉE'S SINGING GROUP WOULD BE PERFORMING THAT NIGHT. SHE FOUND SOME FRIENDS WHO SAT FRONT AND CENTER TO THE STAGE AND JOINED THEIR CIRCLE. ONE OF THE FRIENDS IN THE SISTER CIRCLE WAS NOT ONLY A MEMBER OF A SOCIAL CLUB THEY BOTH BELONGED TO, BUT ALSO A SISTER IN CHRIST WHO WENT TO THE SAME CHURCH FOR THE LAST SEVERAL YEARS, SO SHE FELT SHE WAS IN GREAT COMPANY WITH THESE BEAUTIFUL LADIES.

THE NIGHT ONLY CONTINUED TO BE MORE MAGICAL AS THE LEAD SINGER JOHNNIE HARRIS AND HIS GROUP PERFORMED A BEAUTIFUL LOVE BALLAD BY SMOKEY ROBINSON TITLED OOO BABY BABY DOWN ON THEIR KNEES IN FRONT OF HER. HIS VOICE WAS SO SMOOTH, SULTRY AND SEXY AS HE PERFORMED THE SONG WITH USUAL PERFECTION.

HIS VOICE WAS TRULY FIRST TENOR AND THE NOTES MELTED FROM HIS THROAT LIKE HONEY. SHE COULD FEEL EVERY NOTE RADIATING IN HER HEART AND SHE KNEW WITHOUT A DOUBT, THIS SONG WAS MEANT TO BE FROM HIM TO HER IN THE FORM OF A HEARTFELT, SOULFUL APOLOGY FOR THE LOST RELATIONSHIP THAT ALMOST ENDED IN MARRIAGE TO JOHNNIE HARRIS.

IT MADE HER REMINISCE FOR JUST A BRIEF MOMENT. FROM SOMEWHERE DEEP INSIDE SHE FELT AN OVERWHELMING URGE TO RELEASE ALL THE PENT UP, HORMONAL ENERGY

THAT HAD TAKEN OVER HER BODY ALL NIGHT. EARLIER, SHE FELT A RUSH OF NOSTALGIA AND EMOTIONS SO STRONG, THEY HAD DRIVEN HER HEART, MIND, SOUL, AND BODY TO A PLACE THAT WAS UNFAMILIAR AND QUITE SCARY. UNKNOWN TERRITORY, THAT WAS COMING FROM THE INSIDE OF HER VERY SOUL.

BEFORE SHE COULD STOP HERSELF, SHE GRABBED HER HANDBAG AND COAT AND RAN TO HER CAR EVEN BEFORE THE GROUP HAD FINISHED THEIR SECOND SET. ONCE SAFELY LOCKED INSIDE, SHE BROKE DOWN AND ALLOWED HER EMOTIONS TO TAKE CONTROL OF HER HEART. SHE WEPT FOR HER PART IN THE SEPARATION OF THE RELATIONSHIP THAT SHOULD HAVE ULTIMATELY RESULTED IN MARRIAGE. AND SHE WEPT FOR THE HEARTBREAK SHE CAUSED HIM WHEN SHE SO ABRUPTLY ENDED THE RELATIONSHIP AND MARRIED SOMEONE ELSE NOT REALIZING AT THE TIME THE PAIN, SHE HAD CAUSED HIM.

SHE REALIZED NOW THAT MORE COMMUNICATION WAS DESPERATELY NEEDED IN THIS CONNECTION BECAUSE SHE ALLOWED RUMORS OF HIS INFIDELITIES AND WOMANIZING BEHAVIORS TO PLAY A LARGE ROLE IN HER DECISION TO END THINGS AND WALK AWAY TO THE ARMS OF A PAST TEEN-AGE LOVER. ONCE SHE BECAME AWARE OF THE VITAL ROLE SHE PLAYED IN THE DESTRUCTION OF THE RELATIONSHIP, RHEA GAVE HERSELF THE PERMISSION SHE NEEDED TO RELEASE AND BREAK FREE AS SHE WEPT LIKE A NEWBORN BABY UNTIL SHE WAS PURGED AND DEPLETED OF ALL THE PENT-UP TEARS SHE'D BEEN HARBORING.

CHAPTER 4

THE COMMUNITY BLOCK EVENT

August 3 was a beautiful sunny day in Mahogany Valley, Ohio. Rhea navigated the classy Mocha colored Cadillac SRX Luxury Edition expertly through the parked cars which were already becoming packed in the small spaces that were designated as temporary parking areas. She turned to her long-time childhood friend Candy and both ladies did a last minute make up check before exiting the vehicle. They made a few minor feminine adjustments then both ladies were ready to go.

AS RHEA EXITED THE DRIVER'S SIDE, SHE WAS APPROACHED BY A NICE GENTLEMAN WHO EXPLAINED THAT HE WAS PART OF A POPULAR BAND THERE IN TOWN, AND THAT HE AND HIS FELLOW BAND MEMBERS WOULD BE PLAYING AT THIS EVENT, AND LATER HEADING OVER TO A POPULAR NIGHT SPOT IN TOWN. HE SAID HE SPOTTED HER FROM HIS TRUCK, AND HE WANTED TO INVITE HER TO COME AND HEAR THEM PLAY.

RHEA WAVED FOR CANDY TO GO AHEAD SO SHE DID NOT HAVE TO WAIT UNTIL THE GENTLEMAN FINISHED WITH HIS CONVERSATION. HE CONTINUED TO DETAIN HER UNTIL SHE AGREED TO COME OUT AND HEAR HIM PLAY THAT EVENING. RHEA POLITELY AGREED TO COME AND HEAR THE BAND PLAY WHICH SEEMED TO SATISFY HIM ENOUGH TO LET HER PASS. SHE HAD HEARD ONLY GOOD THINGS ABOUT THE BAND AND SECRETLY SHE WAS ANXIOUS TO SEE WHAT ALL THE RUMORS WERE ABOUT SURROUNDING THEM.

RHEA BEGAN TO WALK FAST TO TRY AND CATCH UP TO CANDY. THEY BOTH NOTICED HOW MUCH THE AIR WAS THICK WITH THE SMELL OF SEVERAL VENDOR FOOD TRUCKS COOKING AND SELLING VARIOUS CULINARY DELIGHTS WHICH MADE HER THINK ABOUT HOW SHE AND CANDY HAD BEEN SO HAPPY TO SEE EACH OTHER AFTER SO MANY YEARS, THEY'D BOTH FORGOTTEN TO GRAB ANYTHING TO EAT. NOW THEY WERE BOTH STARVING AND ANXIOUS TO TRY SOME OF THE VARIOUS DISHES THAT WERE OFFERED. SHE WOULD MOST DEFINITELY HAVE TO TRY SOME OF THE DELICIOUS SMELLING BARBEQUE WHICH WAS ONE OF HER MOST FAVORITE FOODS IN THE WORLD.

SUDDENLY, RHEA SPOTTED HER GIRLFRIEND NOVA WAVING FROM ONE OF THE PICNIC TABLES WHERE SHE AND HER FAMILY WAITED AND SAVED SEATS FOR THEM. THE EVENT WAS SET UP IN BLOCK PARTY STYLE WITH SEVERAL BLOCKS PARTICIPATING AS THEY DID EVERY YEAR. THIS YEAR WAS JUST AS POPULAR AS THE PAST

ONES WITH FAMILIAR FACES GATHERED FROM ALL FOUR SIDES OF TOWN AND SOME FROM NEARBY CITIES SUCH AS COLUMBUS, CLEVELAND, AKRON AND EVEN NEW YORK.

PEOPLE WERE LAUGHING, TALKING, AND EMBRACING ONE ANOTHER BECAUSE SOME HAD GROWN UP TOGETHER AS CHILDREN BUT, HAD NOT SEEN EACH OTHER FOR MANY YEARS AND WERE GENUINELY HAPPY TO RECONNECT AFTER SO LONG. THE SCENE REMINDED RHEA OF THE AFRICAN AMERICAN FAMILY REUNION WHICH WAS ORIGINATED TO HONOR BLACK HERITAGE AND STRENGTHEN THE BLACK FAMILY.

TO HER, IT WAS A BEAUTIFUL SIGHT TO SEE, AND SHE GAVE KUDOS TO THE COMMITTEE WHO SPONSORED IT EACH YEAR. RHEA AND CANDY APPROACHED THE TABLE WHERE HER FRIEND BECKONED. AT THAT MOMENT, RHEA SUDDENLY SPOTTED NOVA'S BROTHER JOHNNIE HARRIS WITH THE VOICE LIKE SILKY SATIN WHO HAD

SERENADED HER WITH HIS GROUP AT THE BOULEVARD CAFE.

RHEA'S INTUITION KICKED IN AT THAT MOMENT WHICH HAD HER TURNING TO HER LEFT AND STARING DIRECTLY AT RICO WHO HAD EYES ON HER WHILE TALKING TO A FRIEND. SHE COULDN'T QUITE UNDERSTAND WHY THE AIR AROUND HER BECAME SO THIN WHICH MADE IT DIFFICULT TO BREATHE. SHE IMMEDIATELY PULLED A FANCY FAN FROM HER PURSE TO HELP HER WITH THE DISCOMFORT. FOR THE TIME BEING, SHE WAS GOING TO TRY TO CALM THE FLAMES THAT HAD ERUPTED SO ABRUPTLY IN HER LADY PARTS.

WITH JOHNNIE ON HER RIGHT AND RICO ON HER LEFT, RHEA NEEDED MORE THAN HER FOLDED FAN TO COOL DOWN. GOD THIS HAS GOT TO STOP, SHE MURMURED TO HERSELF AS SHE TURNED AWAY TO TALK WITH HER FRIENDS FOR DISTRACTION AND TO CATCH UPON THE LATEST NEWS IN THE VALLEY.

As time went on, Rhea and Candy went to find food for the group at the table. They placed their orders and found seats to wait until their meals were ready. On the way back, Rico approached them and the three took pictures together. Just as Rhea turned to leave, he grabbed her arm gently and again the ever so soft whisper in her ear inquiring as to where she would be later after the event?

She didn't hesitate to tell him about the invitation from the band member earlier which she fully intended to honor. Just as she was about to walk away, he stopped her again. This time requesting, she not leave the block party without making absolute sure she left her cell number with him. By now, the temperature felt like it had been turned up to 200 degrees.

SHE QUICKLY PROMISED SHE WOULD AS SHE HURRIEDLY PUT DISTANCE BETWEEN THEM. SHE JOINED HER FRIENDS AT THE TABLE FOR LUNCH AND SOMEHOW MANAGED TO RETRIEVE A NOTE FROM HER PURSE UNNOTICED, TO WRITE HER NUMBER ON. AFTER LUNCH SHE MANAGED TO SLIP IT TO HIM WHILE THE OTHER'S ATTENTIONS WERE ELSEWHERE. SHE WONDERED IF WHEN SHE HEARD FROM HIM WOULD SHE EVEN RESPOND OR CONTINUE TO RUN AND HIDE? SHE DIDN'T BEGIN TO KNOW THE ANSWER TO THAT QUESTION SHE WOULD JUST HAVE TO WAIT AND SEE.

CHAPTER 5

GIRLS NIGHT OUT

RHEA GOT DRESSED FOR THE EVENING IN A YELLOW CALVIN KLEIN NUMBER THAT CLUNG TIGHT TO HER WAIST AND SPREAD OUT WIDE BELOW THE HIPS. SHE PAIRED IT WITH A SHORT JACKET WITH THE SAME YELLOW, TAN AND BROWN PRINT, AND LARGE GOLD EARRINGS, WITH AN AFRICAN NECKLACE AND BRACELET THAT WAS LARGE AND IMPRESSIVE.

SHE WORE TAN SLINGBACK PUMPS AND A SHIMMERY GOLD HEAD BAND AROUND HER BLACK CURLS. ONCE SHE WAS READY, SHE HEADED OUT TO PICK UP CANDY WHO LOOKED ADORABLE IN A BLACK PLEATED

SKIRT WITH MATCHING SWEATER AND TOP. BLACK STOCKINGS AND PUMPS COMPLETED HER ENSEMBLE. BOTH LADIES LOOKED READY TO STIR UP TROUBLE WHEREVER THEY LANDED TONIGHT.

AS THEY ENTERED THE CLUB'S PARKING LOT, THEY SPOTTED ANOTHER FRIEND FROM CHILDHOOD WHICH NEITHER LADY HAD SEEN FOR MANY YEARS. THEY ALL LAUGHED AND TALKED AND CONSIDERED TONIGHT A GOOD OMEN TO HAVE BUMPED INTO EACH OTHER AFTER SO MANY YEARS OF BEING APART. THEY WOULD SURELY HAVE MUCH TO SHARE WITH EACH OTHER SINCE THEIR ADULT LIVES HAD LED THEM ALL ON SUCH DIFFERENT PATHS.

THE LADIES FOUND SEATS IN THE SMALL LOUNGE THAT WAS NEAR WHERE THE BAND WAS PLAYING. RHEA SPOTTED THE GENTLEMAN WHO HAD EXTENDED THE INVITATION PLAYING LEAD GUITAR UP FRONT. AS SHE LOOKED IN HIS DIRECTION, HE

GREETED HER WITH A SMILE AND A WAVE. SHE POLITELY SMILED AND WAVED BACK AS SHE FOUND HERSELF A SEAT.

RHEA WONDERED HOW ALL THESE PEOPLE FIT INTO THE SMALL SPACE WHERE THE BAR WAS MORE THAN HALF OF THE FLOOR SPACE AND THE BAND FIT ONTO THE OTHER HALF WHICH LEFT VERY LITTLE ROOM FOR MUCH ELSE EXCEPT MAYBE A FEW SCATTERED TABLES AND CHAIRS WHEREVER THEY FIT.

JUST THEN, RHEA NOTICED JOHNNIE HARRIS. HE CAME OVER AND SPOKE AND BOUGHT A ROUND OF DRINKS FOR HER AND HER FRIENDS LIKE THE GENTLEMAN HE WAS. WITH DRINKS IN HAND, THE LADIES SAT BACK TO ENJOY THE MUSIC AND CONVERSATION AMONGST THEMSELVES.

SUDDENLY, RHEA FELT THE HAIRS ON THE BACK OF HER NECK STAND UP AND KNEW INSTINCTIVELY THAT "HE" MUST BE SOMEWHERE NEARBY. ALL

AT ONCE THERE HE WAS SLIDING INTO THE BOOTH WHERE SHE AND CANDY SAT. HE IMMEDIATELY REACHED OVER AND PLACED HIS ARM AROUND HER NECK WHILE GENTLY WHISPERING IN HER EAR.

AGAIN, ALL THE AIR IN THE ROOM SEEMED TO GO AT ONCE AND SHE WAS LEFT GASPING FOR BREATH. SHE OFFERED TO BUY HIM A DRINK JUST SO THEY COULD MOVE TO THE BAR WHERE THERE WOULD BE MORE AIR. RHEA AND RICO MADE THEIR WAY TO THE BAR WHERE HE STOOD SLIGHTLY BEHIND HER.

FEELING QUITE NAUGHTY AND ACKNOWLEDGING THE FULL HEATED FURNACE SHE CALLED A BODY; SHE DECIDED TO TEMPT FATE AND PLAY A LITTLE WITH FIRE. RHEA STRATEGICALLY AND DELIBERATELY BENT OVER BRUSHING UP AGAINST HIM SLIGHTLY TO SEE IF SHE HAD THE DESIRED EFFECT ON HIM BY STANDING SO CLOSE WHILE WAITING FOR THE WAITRESS TO SERVE THEIR DRINKS.

SHE SMILED WICKEDLY AFTER FEELING HER LITTLE TRICK MOST DEFINITELY WORKED. THAT MADE HER WANT TO UNDRESS HIM AND INVESTIGATE RIGHT THEN AND THERE. INSTEAD, SHE SMILED WITH A MISCHIEVOUS TWINKLE IN HER EYES AS SHE TURNED TO FACE HIM.

AT THAT MOMENT, THE TWO STOPPED, AND STARED, INTO EACH OTHER'S EYES WITH SUCH STRONG INTENSITY IT SEEMED THE WHOLE WORLD HAD SUDDENLY DISAPPEARED LEAVING ONLY THE TWO OF THEM, WITH EYES FROZEN ON EACH OTHER IN ITS EXISTENCE.

RHEA FELT AS IF SHE WERE IN A MOVIE WHERE ALL THE MAIN CHARACTERS WERE MOVING IN SLOW MOTION AS IF THEY WERE UNDER WATER. RICO STARED INTO HER EYES FOR A MOMENT THEN GAVE HER HIS AWARD-WINNING SMILE. THE ONE THAT MADE HER WHOLE-BODY ACHE WITH THE ICY COLD TOUCH OF WINTER AND THE

HEATED FLAMES OF A DOZEN FIRES BLAZING ALL AT ONCE.

GOOD GRACIOUS, SHE WHISPERED TO HERSELF KNOWING THAT AT THAT VERY MOMENT IN TIME SHE WOULD HAVE NO CHOICE BUT TO EXPLORE THESE FEELINGS SHE FELT FOR HIM. RHEA ALSO RECOGNIZED THE FACT THAT ONLY HE WOULD BE THE ONE TO EXTINGUISH THE FIRE THAT RAGED IN HER WHOLE ENTIRE BODY FROM HEAD TOE.

CHAPTER 6

SEPTEMBER LOVE

Rico took his own sweet time bringing her body to a feverish pitch. "Rico please" she begged for release but Rico continued to tease and taunt her. Rhea lost all reasoning and was totally gripped by such ecstasy she was never even aware that she was calling his name repeatedly.

Rico held her so tightly to his body she could barely breathe. She buried her face against his chest as he cradled her head in both hands and held her tightly to him.

RICO'S BREATHING THEN BECAME SHALLOWER AND MORE LABORED. STILL, HE CLUNG TO RHEA SEEMINGLY UNABLE TO LET GO AS THE EARTH-SHATTERING LOVEMAKING CAME TO A SLOW ENDING. BOTH TWINS WERE RELUCTANT TO LET EACH OTHER GO. AFTERWARDS.....

AFTER THAT NIGHT, THE TWO TALKED BRIEFLY ON THE PHONE FOR A FEW WEEKS. THEY LAUGHED AND JOKED TOGETHER A LOT UNTIL THEY FINALLY MADE A DATE TO GET TOGETHER. THE RESTAURANT IN PENNSYLVANIA WAS SIMI-CROWDED WHICH DIDN'T BOTHER EITHER ONE WHO ONLY HAD EYES FOR EACH OTHER. RICO LIKED THIS RESTAURANT BECAUSE IT HAD A FULL-SERVICE BAR INSIDE, AND IT WAS ATTACHED TO A BEAUTIFUL MARRIOTT HOTEL.

ALTHOUGH RICO LIKED THIS SPOT, HE'D ONLY FREQUENTED IT ONCE OR TWICE IN THE PAST WHEN THE LADY HE WAS WITH WAS SPECIAL. HE HAD NO EMOTIONAL CONNECTIONS TO RHEA

YET, BUT THE PHYSICAL ATTRACTION, CHEMISTRY OR WHATEVER IT WAS CALLED, WAS DRIVING HIM INSANE AND HE DID NOT WANT TO WAIT A DAY LONGER TO HAVE THIS WOMAN AND HE MEANT TO HAVE EVERY INCH OF HER LUSCIOUS BODY ALL NIGHT LONG.

AFTER DINNER, THEY DECIDED TO HEAD STRAIGHT TO THE ROOM WHICH HAD ALREADY BEEN ARRANGED AHEAD OF TIME BECAUSE RICO HAD REQUESTED ONE WITH A JACUZZI TUB INSIDE AND THOSE USUALLY WERE THE FIRST TO BE BOOKED. HE HAD PLANNED EVERYTHING OUT EXACTLY RIGHT AND PRAYED THE NIGHT WOULD PROVE TO BE WORTH ALL HIS EFFORTS.

THERE WAS A BEAUTIFUL BOUQUET OF WHITE CHOCOLATE ROSES (SOME OF RHEA'S FAVORITES) HE'D FOUND OUT FROM THE PHONE CONVERSATIONS THEY'D HAD PRIOR. PETALS WERE SPRINKLED ON THE BED AND ALSO IN THE JACUZZI TUB WHICH RICO HAD

CALLED AND REQUESTED THE HOTEL HAVE READY UPON THEIR ARRIVAL.

EVERYTHING SEEMED IN ORDER, AND HE COULDN'T WAIT TO GET THE REST OF THE NIGHT STARTED. RHEA SAT DOWN SLOWLY ONTO THE LARGE KING-SIZED BED FEELING AS IF SHE WERE BACK IN HIGH SCHOOL WHEN SHE FIRST LOST HER VIRGINITY. SHE WASN'T AFRAID OF COURSE SHE WAS A GROWN WOMAN WITH A FEW LONG-TERM RELATIONSHIPS BEHIND HER BUT, THIS FEELING WAS NEW, AND SHE WOULD HAVE TO LEARN TO CONTROL IT, ONCE SHE FIGURED OUT WHAT "IT," ACTUALLY WAS.

RICO SAT BESIDE HER AND PLACED HIS ARM AROUND HER NECK AS HE'D DONE ON THE NIGHT AT THE LOUNGE. HE SPOKE VERY SOFTLY ASKING IF SHE WERE AFRAID OF HIM? SHE ANSWERED NO AND TURNED TO FACE HIM. HE THEN TOOK THIS OPPORTUNITY TO KISS HER SOFTLY AT FIRST, AND THEN MORE INTENSELY. AS THE PASSION BETWEEN THE TWO

BEGAN TO IGNITE A FIRE IN BOTH LOVERS, THE FONDLING BECAME HEAVIER, AND MORE PASSIONATE THE KISSING GREW. THEY EXPLORED EACH OTHER'S MOUTHS, SUCKING TONGUES, LIPS, EAR LOBES, NECKS. HOT, STEAMY, KISSES THAT LED TO HEAVY BREATHING AND GROPING HANDS.

THE COUPLE TOOK THEIR TIME AND UNDRESSED EACH OTHER. RICO TOOK HIS TIME APPRECIATING ALL THE BEAUTY THIS WOMAN HAD BEEN BLESSED WITH. HE STARED FOR A FEW MINUTES THEN MOVED BACK A LITTLE TO GET A BETTER VIEW OF HER ENTIRE BODY.

RHEA ASKED IF SOMETHING WERE WRONG BECAUSE TO HER, HE ACTED AS IF HE NO LONGER WANTED TO TOUCH HER WHICH MADE HER FEEL UNCOMFORTABLE OR THAT SHE HAD TURNED HIM OFF SOMEHOW. INSTANTLY, RICO ASSURED HER THAT EVERYTHING ABOUT HER WAS PLEASING AND DESIRABLE TO HIM,

BUT HE WANTED TO TAKE HIS TIME AND NOT RUSH HER. SECRETLY, HE WAS TAKING HIS TIME TO GET CONTROL OF THE RAGING FIRE HE WAS FEELING FOR HER. AFTERWARD, THEY BOTH LAY SIDE BY SIDE WAITING FOR THEIR HEARTRATES TO GO DOWN AND A NORMAL BREATHING RHYTHM TO RESUME.

CHAPTER 7

THE DIVINE TWINS A SOUL CONTRACT

BOTH RHEA AND RICO REALIZED THAT WHAT HAD TRANSPIRED BETWEEN THEM THAT DAY AT THE MARRIOTT HOTEL WAS NOT YOUR NORMAL EVERYDAY ROMP IN THE HAY AS THEY SAY. RHEA HAD LEFT THAT NEXT MORNING THINKING SHE WOULD NEVER SLEEP WITH HIM AGAIN FOR FEAR SHE WOULD LOSE SELF-CONTROL OVER SEX. IN OTHER WORDS, SHE FELT SHE WAS ENTIRELY TOO OLD TO GET "D$%&*-MATIZED" AS THEY WOULD SAY IN HER SISTER CIRCLE.

ON THE OTHER HAND, RICO LEFT THE HOTEL THAT MORNING WITH HIS MIND ON WHEN THE NEXT SEXUAL ENCOUNTER BETWEEN THEM WOULD BE? HE WAS HOOKED, AND THAT WAS EXTREMELY HARD TO DO WITH HIM. HE WAS THE LOVE-EM AND LEAVE- EM AND ON TO THE NEXT CONQUEST KIND OF GUY. HE WAS ALWAYS NON-COMMITTAL AND EMOTIONALLY UNAVAILABLE WHEN IT CAME TO RELATIONSHIPS WITH WOMEN.

HOWEVER, HE HAD TO ADMIT THAT SOMETHING MAGICAL HAPPENED THAT NIGHT IN THAT HOTEL ROOM WHICH HE HADN'T EVER EXPERIENCED BEFORE AND QUITE FRANKLY, HE WAS UNDECIDED AS TO WHETHER HE SHOULD TRY SEX WITH HER EVER AGAIN. IT WAS FIRE AND IT WAS ALSO ICE AT THE SAME TIME. AND FOR THE FIRST TIME IN HIS ADULT LIFE, HE WAS A LITTLE AFRAID OF THE FEELINGS HE FELT FOR A WOMAN.

RICO WASN'T ACCUSTOMED TO INVOLVING EMOTIONS OR FEELINGS

INTO HIS SEXUAL ENCOUNTERS BECAUSE HE LIVED BY THE MOTO THAT SEX WAS SEX AND AS TINA TURNER'S HIT SONG SAID, "WHAT'S LOVE GOT TO DO WITH IT?" BUT WHAT HE WAS FEELING FOR THIS LADY LAST NIGHT AND EVEN NOW, HE JUST SIMPLY COULD NOT EXPLAIN. SO, HE DECIDED THAT HE SHOULD TRY IT ONE MORE TIME TO SEE WHETHER THE FEELINGS WERE REAL OR TOO MANY LONG ISLAND ICE TEAS THAT NIGHT.

RHEA BEING THE LIFE-LONG SCHOLAR SHE WAS DECIDED TO RESEARCH WHAT INTENSE, SUPER POWERFUL LOVE MAKING BETWEEN ADULTS MEANT. AS SHE READ, SHE BEGAN TO UNRAVEL THE MYSTERY OF THE SITUATION THAT HAD KEPT HER UP WONDERING ON SO MANY NIGHTS AFTER THEIR FIRST SEXUAL ENCOUNTER. SHE READ THAT A SOUL MATE, CAN BE ANYONE WHO MIGHT BE SENT INTO YOUR LIFE TO TEACH YOU OR YOU TO TEACH THEM A LESSON FOR A TIME OR A SEASON.

SHE CONTINUED TO READ THAT A TWIN FLAME IS MORE LIKE THE OTHER HALF OF YOUR SOUL. A SINGLE SOUL SPLIT ACROSS TWO BODIES. A TWIN FLAME CONNECTION IS THE TOUGHEST KIND OF CONNECTION BECAUSE OFTEN THE TWO HAVE LIVED VASTLY DIFFERENT LIVES UNTIL THEY COME INTO UNION WHICH IS DIVINELY GUIDED AND DIRECTED BY GOD.

RHEA CONTINUED TO READ AND STUDY THAT TWIN FLAMES ARE UNDER A SOUL CONTRACT AND THAT ANYONE OR ANYTHING THAT TRIES TO STOP THE CONNECTION WILL BE DEALT WITH THROUGH KARMA. YIKES, SHE THOUGHT, THIS STUFF IS TOO DEEP, BUT IT MADE SENSE IN A WAY BECAUSE THE CONNECTION BETWEEN HER AND RICO COULD NOT BE EXPLAINED ANY OTHER WAY. SHE MADE UP HER MIND RIGHT THEN AND THERE TO RUN. SHE SIMPLY HAD TO STAY AWAY FROM HIM NO MATTER WHAT. LITTLE DID SHE KNOW THAT THE UNIVERSE HAD MADE OTHER PLANS FOR THIS UNION AND NEITHER SHE NOR RICO HAD BEEN CONSULTED.

CHAPTER 8

THE CHASE

AFTER THE ONE GLORIOUS NIGHT SPENT WITH RICO, RHEA DECIDED IT WAS SIMPLY TIME TO RUN FROM THIS SITUATION. SHE COULD NOT EXPLAIN THE FEELINGS THAT WAS STIRRING ON HER INSIDE AND OUT. ALL SHE KNEW WAS THAT IN ALL HER PAST RELATIONSHIPS, NONE HAD EVER FELT THIS INTENSE OR SCARY. SCARY BECAUSE SHE COULD NOT CONTROL HER EMOTIONS AROUND HIM.

THE ONE THING SHE HAD ALWAYS PRIDED HERSELF ON WAS HER ABILITY TO CONTROL EMOTIONS IN HER RELATIONSHIPS EVEN WHEN SHE FELT VERY EMOTIONAL. BUT WITH HIM, SHE

DIDN'T HAVE A CLUE AS TO WHY HER HEARTBEAT SO FAST AND EVERY PART OF HER BECAME HOT AS IF A MATCH HAD BEEN LIT INSIDE OF HER, AND NOTHING MADE SENSE ANYMORE.

RHEA JUSTIFIED HER RUNNING FROM RICO AS THE ONLY OPTION UNTIL SHE COULD GET A FIRM GRIP AND SOME SELF-CONTROL ON THIS SITUATION. ON THE OTHER HAND, RICO CALLED MANY TIMES OVER THE NEXT SEVERAL WEEKS BUT WAS UNSUCCESSFUL IN MAKING ANY CONTACT. HE WONDERED IF HE'D DONE SOMETHING WRONG TO OFFEND HER BUT COULDN'T FIGURE OUT WHAT IT MIGHT BE BECAUSE THEIR DATE WAS OFF THE CHARTS, LITERALLY, AND HE KNEW SHE'D FELT IT TOO BY THE WAY SHE SMILED AND RESTED HER HEAD ON HIS CHEST FOR THE NIGHT.

RICO REMINISCED ABOUT HOW RHEA HAD FALLEN ASLEEP LAYING ON HIS CHEST, AND HE TOO HAD FALLEN ASLEEP HOLDING HER TIGHT TO HIM AS IF HE NEVER WANTED TO LET HER GO.

To Rico, the night was magical, and he couldn't wait to see her again and try to recapture the magic they'd shared on that first night.

After so many unanswered calls, Rico simply could not take it anymore, so he got into his truck and drove by her home to see if her car was there. When he saw that she was home, he went a few blocks down, pulled over, and called her mobile phone again. This time he left a message that would surely get her attention if nothing else. He said listen baby, I just drove past your house, and I see your car is there, so I know you're home. Now if you do not answer your phone, I will be forced to come knocking on your door until I get an answer.

She called back within moments of the message asking how he was and how he knew where she lived because she hadn't told him. He

TOLD HER THAT HE HAD FOLLOWED HER HOME ONE NIGHT TO MAKE SURE SHE WAS SAFE. SHE DISMISSED THE QUESTION AND GOT RIGHT TO THE POINT KNOWING SHE OWED HIM SOME FORM OF AN EXPLANATION ABOUT HER ELUSIVE BEHAVIOR. THIS WAS A CONVERSATION SHE DREADED HAVING WITH HIM BUT PULLED UP HER BIG GIRL PANTIES ANYWAY AND DOVE RIGHT IN.

SHE KNEW SHE WOULD ALWAYS TELL RICO THE TRUTH BECAUSE SHE WAS A WOMAN WHO HATED LIES AND COULD NOT TOLERATE THEM SO SHE TRIED HER ABSOLUTE BEST TO ALWAYS TELL THE TRUTH AND LET THE CHIPS FALL WHERE THEY MAY. SHE EXPLAINED THAT SHE HAD BEEN THINKING A LOT ABOUT THEIR CONNECTION AND SIMPLY SLOWED THINGS DOWN BEFORE THEY WENT TOO FAR TOO FAST. RHEA SAID THAT MAYBE IT WASN'T A GOOD IDEA TO CONTINUE SEEING EACH OTHER AND THAT THEY SHOULD CALL THINGS OFF RIGHT NOW.

RICO LISTENED TO HER WORDS AND NEVER INTERRUPTED LIKE THE GENTLEMAN HE WAS TAUGHT TO BE WHEN A LADY NEEDED TO GET SOMETHING OFF HER CHEST. WHEN RHEA WAS FINISHED, HE THEN SPOKE. HE TOLD HER THAT WHATEVER THOUGHTS SHE HAD IN HER HEAD ABOUT THE TWO OF THEM WALKING AWAY FROM EACH OTHER WAS SIMPLY NOT AN OPTION. HE SAID IT WAS TOO LATE TO EVEN CONSIDER ANYTHING LIKE THAT AT THIS POINT BUT WAS RELUCTANT TO EXPLAIN WHY. RICO WAS SOMEONE WHO ALSO NEVER SHOWED EMOTIONS BUT AS TIME WOULD EVENTUALLY TELL, SHE WOULD DISCOVER HE WAS EMOTIONALLY UNAVAILABLE TO EVERYONE EXCEPT HER.

CHAPTER 9

THE LOVERS A DIVINE SOUL TIE

Autumn in Mahogany Valley, Ohio came dressed in beautiful colors of reds gold, purple, orange. and yellow, just to name a few. All the foliage around the valley seemed to be alive and vibrant. Rhea drove through her favorite park where she had agreed to meet Rico. He had texted her earlier and explained exactly where he would be waiting for her.

Since neither one of them had eaten dinner yet she decided to surprise him with a picnic

BASKET FULL OF GOODIES. SHE BROUGHT CHICKEN WINGS AND ROLLS MAC SALAD AND BAKED BEANS AND FOR DESSERT LITTLE MINI PEACH COBBLERS, WHICH WERE HIS FAVORITE. SHE HAD CHILLED HIS FAVORITE DRINK AND BROUGHT TWO BLANKETS AND A TABLECLOTH FOR FULL EFFECT.

RHEA FOUND RICO IN THE PERFECT SPOT UNDER A TREE THAT WAS LARGE ENOUGH TO PROVIDE SHADE AND HIDDEN FROM PEOPLE WHO MIGHT BE VISITING THE PARK AND IN THE SAME AREA AS THEY WERE. RICO TOOK EVERYTHING FROM HER HANDS AND HELPED HER SET UP FOR THEIR LITTLE ROMANTIC FEAST. RICO WAS BLOWN AWAY AT THE THOUGHTFULNESS THAT RHEA HAD SHOWN IN TAKING TIME TO BRING SOME OF HIS FAVORITE DRINKS AND FOOD THAT SMELLED AMAZING.

RICO TURNED ON HIS MOBILE PHONE AND PLAYED MUSIC THAT WAS SENSUOUS AND FAMILIAR. THE EARLY DINNER WAS RIGHT ON TIME AND HIT

THE SPOT WHICH HAD THE LOVERS RELAXED AND SATISFIED. THE COUPLE LEANED BACK AGAINST THE TREE AND TALKED ABOUT FUTURE, REMINISCED ABOUT THE PAST, AND FELT GRATEFUL FOR THE PRESENT.

RICO LEANED OVER AND KISSED HER GENTLY WHILE WHISPERING SOFTLY IN HER EAR. COME WITH ME HE URGED, LEAVING RHEA CURIOUS AS TO WHAT HE HAD IN MIND NOW.

HE HELPED HER TO HER FEET, WRAPPED THE BLANKET AROUND HER, AND LED HER TO A ROUND WHITE GAZEBO WHICH WAS LESS THAN THREE FEET AWAY. HE VERY GENTLY LEANED RHEA AGAINST THE GAZEBO WHILE CONTINUING TO WHISPER SWEET SOOTHING WORDS IN HER EAR. THE WORDS HE WHISPERED WERE ALL TRUE AND HE HAD TO ADMIT TO HIMSELF THAT HER BODY TURNED HIM ON LIKE NO ONE ELSE COULD AND THE LOVEMAKING BETWEEN HIM AND HER WAS FIRE. RICO CONTINUED MAKING SLOW PASSIONATE LOVE TO

HER WHILE HOLDING HER SECURELY IN BOTH OF HIS STRONG ARMS.

THIS FEELING WAS UNFAMILIAR WHICH MADE HIM FEEL UNEASY ABOUT THE WHOLE SITUATION. HOWEVER, HE STILL, HAD TO ADMIT AND COULD NOT DENY, THE STRONG, BINDING, CONNECTION BETWEEN THE TWO OF THEM. THEY HELD ON TO EACH OTHER AND STARED DEEPLY INTO ONE ANOTHER'S EYES AS WAVES OF PLEASURE TOOK THEM TO HEIGHTS TOO DELICIOUS TO BELIEVE.

FINALLY, THE COUPLE BOTH ACHIEVED THEIR DESIRED TARGET TOGETHER. THE SHEER INTENSITY COUPLED WITH MIND-BLOWING PASSION ROCKED RICO TO THE CORE CAUSING HIM TO FALL TO HIS KNEES DROPPING ONTO THE SOFT GRASS BENEATH THEIR FEET WHILE STILL HOLDING RHEA WITH BOTH HANDS. AFTERWARD, BOTH LAY SPENT, DAZED, AND CONFUSED WONDERING WHAT JUST HAPPENED TO THEM AGAIN?

NEITHER RICO NOR RHEA WERE AWARE THAT WHAT HAD JUST OCCURRED COULD ONLY HAPPEN BETWEEN TWO PEOPLE WHO SHARED ONE SOUL THAT HAD BEEN SPLIT INTO TWO AND BROUGHT BACK TOGETHER BY DIVINE DESTINY. THIS UNION WAS DIVINELY PLANNED, DIVINELY ORCHESTRATED, AND DIVINELY GUIDED AND NOTHING AND NO ONE COULD STOP IT.

CHAPTER 10

A CHANGE IN LOVE

AFTER THE DAY SPENT TOGETHER IN THE PARK THE TWO BECAME INSEPARABLE. THEY MET TWICE A WEEK AND SOMETIMES MORE. MOSTLY EVERY TIME THEY SAW EACH OTHER AND SPENT TIME TOGETHER THE DATE ENDED IN SOME FORM OF A MIND-BLOWING LOVEMAKING SESSION. SOMETIMES, HE INITIATED IT AND SOMETIMES SHE DID BUT WHOMEVER SUGGESTED IT, BOTH WERE VERY EAGER TO OBLIGE.

DAYS AHEAD WERE EXCITING AS THE COUPLE EXPLORED EACH OTHER'S BODIES AND MADE LOVE BOTH INSIDE AND OUTSIDE OR WHEREVER THEY

FOUND A GOOD, ISOLATED SPOT TO TAKE ADVANTAGE OF. THEY SEEMED TO HAVE FORMED A ROUTINE OF CALLING EACH OTHER A FEW TIMES DURING THE DAY WHILE AT WORK JUST TO HEAR EACH OTHER'S VOICES.

DURING THE NEXT MONTHS THAT FOLLOWED, THINGS CHANGED ABRUPTLY FOR THE RELATIONSHIP. RHEA CALLED RICO SEVERAL TIMES A DAY BEFORE HE FINALLY ANSWERED HER CALL. WHEN HE ANSWERED, HE WAS COLD AND DISTANT WHEN HE SPOKE. HE SEEMED IN A HURRY TO HANG UP AND NEVER ANSWERED A DIRECT QUESTION.

HE AVOIDED ANY TALK ABOUT PLANS TO SEE HER AND NOTHING WAS SPOKEN ABOUT THE RELATIONSHIP GOING FORWARD AT ALL. RHEA KNEW INSTINCTIVELY THAT SOMETHING WAS VERY WRONG WITH RICO BUT WHEN ASKED IF THERE WERE A PROBLEM, HE BECAME AGITATED AND ANGRY SO EVENTUALLY SHE JUST GAVE UP. THIS ATTITUDE WENT ON FOR SEVERAL

WEEKS AND DURING HER BIRTHDAY IN NOVEMBER HE WAS NOWHERE TO BE FOUND, AFTER WISHING HER AN ABRUPT HAPPY BIRTHDAY OVER A HURRIED PHONE CALL.

RHEA WAS CONFUSED AND HEARTBROKEN OVER THE CHANGES TO THEIR RELATIONSHIP. THE MAIN REASON SHE WAS SO DISTRAUGHT WAS BECAUSE THINGS HAD SEEMED TO BE HEADING IN A POSITIVE DIRECTION BEFORE THE SUDDEN CHANGE. SHE PLAYED THEIR CONVERSATIONS OVER AND OVER IN HER MIND TRYING TO FIGURE OUT WHAT WENT WRONG. SHE KNEW EXACTLY WHEN THE CHANGE HAPPENED BUT COULD NOT FIGURE OUT WHY IT HAPPENED.

BY THE TIME DECEMBER ROLLED AROUND THERE WAS VERY LITTLE COMMUNICATION BETWEEN THE TWO LOVERS. ON CHRISTMAS DAY SHE RECEIVED A VOICE MAIL WISHING HER AND HER FAMILY A MERRY CHRISTMAS FROM HIM BUT NOTHING MORE. SHE KNEW INSTINCTIVELY AGAIN THAT THIS

WAS THE END OF HER RELATIONSHIP AND SHE NEEDED TO FIND A WAY TO LET RICO GO. RHEA HAD ALWAYS LIVED BY THE MOTO THAT WHEN A LOVE RELATION HAS ENDED IT HAS TO END IN TWO PARTS.

NUMBER 1. YOU MUST LET GO WITH YOUR HEAD. THE BRAIN IS THE CENTRAL LOCATION, AND IT TELLS THE HEART AND THE REST OF THE BODY HOW TO REACT TO THESE FEELINGS, SO IT NEEDS TO BE CONTROLLED FIRST.

NUMBER 2. IS LETTING GO WITH THE HEART. THIS PART IS WAY MORE DIFFICULT TO DO THAN THE FIRST BECAUSE THE HEART WANTS WHAT IT WANTS AND SO DOES THE BODY'S CRAVINGS.

IN THE DAYS AND WEEKS THAT FOLLOWED, SHE SHED MANY TEARS AND SLEEPLESS NIGHTS MOURNING THE LOST RELATIONSHIP. SHE THREW ALL THE ENERGY SHE COULD MUSTER INTO HER WORK. FINALLY, RHEA

DECIDED TO START HAVING GIRL'S NIGHT OUT JUST TO FORGET HER PROBLEMS AND FIND SOME NEW ADVENTURES.

SHE AND TWO FRIENDS WHO CALLED THEMSELVES TRACY, AND TRACIE, WENT OUT ON THE WEEKENDS ABOUT TWICE A MONTH JUST TO HEAR MUSIC, DANCE, AND SEE WHO WAS HANGING OUT. RHEA WOULD ALWAYS BE AVAILABLE AS THE DESIGNATED DRIVER WHEN THE OTHER TWO LADIES ENJOYED A COUPLE OF COCKTAILS FOR THE EVENING. HER ONLY COCKTAILS CONSISTED OF CRANBERRY JUICE AND GINGER ALE.

AT ANY RATE, THE GIRL'S NIGHT OUT EVENINGS HELPED HER TAKE HER MIND OFF HER BROKEN HEART AND ACHING BODY. SHE STILL WISHED SHE KNEW WHAT TRIGGERED THE END OF THE RELATIONSHIP OR WHAT HAPPENED BETWEEN THEM THAT CAUSED SUCH AN ABRUPT AND TOTAL DEPARTURE FROM RICO.

SHE FINALLY MADE UP IN HER MIND THAT THE RELATIONSHIP MUST HAVE SIMPLY RUN ITS COURSE AND THAT HER LOVER HAD GOTTEN EVERYTHING HE'D NEEDED FROM HER, AND THEIR RELATIONSHIP HAD JUST DEPARTED WITHOUT SO MUCH AS A BLIP- BLAM THANK YOU MA'AM EXPLANATION. IN HER OPINION, HE HAD TOTALLY BEHAVED LIKE AN ASS AND IF OR WHEN SHE SAW HIM AGAIN, SHE WOULD MOST DEFINITELY LET HIM KNOW EXACTLY HOW SHE FELT ABOUT HIS BEHAVIOR.

AFTER THE HOLIDAYS, WERE OVER, RHEA COUNTED THE WEEKS SINCE SHE HAD LAST HEARD FROM RICO WITH ANY REAL COMMUNICATION. SHE REALIZED THAT SIX WEEKS HAD GONE BY AND ALTHOUGH THE PAIN HAD DULLED SOME, IT HAD NOT COMPLETELY VANISHED. SHE DECIDED IT WAS ONLY A MATTER OF TIME BEFORE IT BECAME A DISTANT MEMORY. UNTIL THEN, SHE WOULD JUST CONTINUE TO SUFFER IN SILENCE.

CHAPTER 11

A ST. VALENTINE'S DAY REUNION

About a week before the Valentine's Day holiday, Rico called Rhea out of the blue. She was baffled by how the conversation had taken on the old familiar tone and how his mood seemed light and playful like the Rico she had first met. She wondered where this man had been. Why now after all this time had he decided to reach out to her again? And the biggest question was, how was he acting as if nothing happened between them? And that no explanation was needed.

She decided to give him a piece of her mind and ask him if he felt the need to hold a much-needed conversation face to face with her. He declined the invitation and kept acting as if she hadn't blasted him for ghosting her. Rhea decided to let it go for now, but it was far from over for her.

Everyday Rico called her resuming his same position in her life before the tower fell and took her heart with it. Little did she know that the tower moment had affected his life also, and that he'd made a choice that he'd found out was the wrong one leaving him miserable and going crazy missing her and their relationship.

On St. Valentine's Day, Rico called to see what she had planned. He asked if she could meet him and before hanging up, she thought she heard Rico say,

"I Love You!" She quickly hung up the phone as he was saying it thinking it was an accident and it wasn't what he'd said at all. Later, when they met and were talking and looking into each other's eyes, she casually asked if that was what he'd said earlier, he answered yes, I did say I Love You, and I do!

Rhea could hardly believe what she heard but responded truthfully letting him know that she felt the same way. She felt as if the love between them was timeless and so strong no one could ever break their bond. Neither Rhea nor Rico had a clue that the love between them was Divinely given, and had been given over many lifetimes before, but this one was meant to teach them both a lesson before they ascended together for the last time.

Rico made slow, gentle, sweet love to her that day unlike their usual highly passionate lovemaking where they were both hungry and desperate to touch each other. No, this was warm and sensuous, careful and tender. Rico skillfully handled Rhea's body as if she were a virgin. His very own chocolate, satin, doll.

As he made sweet gentle love to her, she held on to him as if she never wanted to let him leave her again. Rico could feel her anxiety towards him and whispered reassuring words to her while planting gentle kisses along her face, forehead, neck and shoulders.

When they were finished, she tried to turn her face away so he wouldn't notice the tears running down her face. But he did notice and reached out and pulled her face into his chest.

HE HELD HER THERE SOOTHING HER AND WHISPERING WORDS OF COMFORT LIKE; SHHHH, AND IT'S ALRIGHT, NO NEED FOR THIS BABY.

BUT ALL RHEA COULD REMEMBER WAS HOW GOOD IT FELT WHEN THEY WERE TOGETHER AND HOW TERRIBLE SHE FELT WHEN HE HAD LEFT HER BEHIND FOR ALL THOSE WEEKS. SHE STILL HAD NO EXPLANATION WHY IT HAPPENED, OR IF AND WHEN IT MIGHT HAPPEN AGAIN. SHE HAD NO CLOSURE WHICH MADE HER FEEL ANXIOUS AND VULNERABLE AND THAT WASN'T A FEELING SHE WAS ACCUSTOMED TO.

AFTER RICO FINALLY GOT HER SETTLED DOWN, HE ASKED IF HE COULD CALL HER FOR THEIR NEXT DATE WHICH LIFTED HER SPIRITS UP TREMENDOUSLY. SHE FELT AS IF THEY WERE FINALLY GETTING BACK ON THE RIGHT PATH. LATER THAT DAY, RHEA DECIDED TO RESEARCH THE WORD SOUL MATES TO SEE IF THE DEFINITION WOULD DESCRIBE THE RELATIONSHIP

BETWEEN HER AND RICO. WHAT SHE FOUND HAD HER ALMOST PARALYZED. NOT ONLY DID SHE FIND SOUL MATES SHE ALSO FOUND SOUL TIES AND SOUL CONTRACTS OF TWIN FLAMES.

SHE KNEW IMMEDIATELY THAT THE TWIN FLAME JOURNEY WAS INDEED THE STORY OF HER AND RICO. SO MANY SIMILARITIES IT WAS UNBELIEVABLE. HER MIND WENT BACK TO LAST FALL WHEN HE KEPT COMING DOWN WITH COLDS AND STOMACH ISSUES THAT EVERY TIME, HE'D GOTTEN ILL, SO DID SHE. AND HOW WHEN HER RIGHT FOOT HAD SWOLLEN FROM GOUT, THE NEXT DAY HE CALLED TO TELL HER HIS LEFT FOOT WAS SWOLLEN WITH GOUT. AND WHEN HE THREW HIS LOWER BACK OUT THE NEXT DAY SHE WAS IN BED WITH HER UPPER BACK OUT. IT WAS UNCANNY HOW THEY BOTH MIRRORED EACH OTHER.

WHEN HE CALLED TO TELL HER, HE WANTED TO SEE HER SHE REMINDED HIM OF ALL THE THINGS THAT

HAPPENED TO THEM THAT MIRRORED EACH OTHER. HE ALSO THOUGHT IT WAS VERY STRANGE AND UNUSUAL THE WAY THEIR BODIES HAD BEEN SO IN SYNC WITH ONE ANOTHER. SHE EXPLAINED THAT SHE LOOKED UP SOUL MATES AND FOUND MORE THAN THAT. SHE TOLD HIM ABOUT THE TWIN FLAME CONNECTION, AND HE LISTENED QUIETLY.

AFTER SHE'D GOTTEN DONE EXPLAINING HE ASKED GENTLY DO YOU THINK THIS IS WHAT WE ARE? WHEN SHE RESPONDED THAT ALL THE CRITERIA FIT, HE HAD TO ADMIT THAT SHE HAD STUMBLED ONTO SOMETHING BUT BECAUSE HE HAD ALWAYS BEEN SOMEONE WITH AN ANALYTICAL MIND, SHE KNEW HE NEEDED TO DO SOME RESEARCH OF HIS OWN. THEY BOTH DID AND WAS AMAZED BY WHAT THEY FOUND.

CHAPTER 12

THE TWIN FLAME JOURNEY DIVINE MASCULINE AND DIVINE FEMININE

ACCORDING TO GARY LITE MERCH

TWIN FLAMES OR TWIN SOULS ARE SAID TO BE THE OTHER HALF OF OUR SOULS. WE EACH HAVE ONLY ONE TWIN AND GENERALLY AFTER BEING SPLIT APART, THE TWO WENT THEIR SEPARATE WAYS AFTER INCARNATING OVER AND OVER AGAIN TO GATHER HUMAN EXPERIENCE BEFORE REUNITING BACK TOGETHER. IDEALLY, THIS HAPPENS IN BOTH OF

THEIR LAST LIFETIMES, SO THEY CAN ASCEND TOGETHER.

THEY BOTH HAVE THE TASK IN POLARITY OF BALANCING THEIR FEMALE AND MALE ASPECTS, AND IDEALLY BECOME ENLIGHTENED BEFORE REUNITING WITH THEIR TWIN FLAME. TWIN FLAMES ARE MAGNETICALLY ATTRACTED TO EACH OTHER. THIS REUNION IS OF TWO COMPLETE AND WHOLE BEINGS. ALL OTHER RELATIONSHIPS THROUGH ALL OUR LIVES ARE SAID TO BE PRACTICE.

A TWIN FLAME OR TWIN SOUL IS THE ONE PERSON WHO YOU FEEL CONNECTED TO ON EVERY LEVEL, NOT JUST ON A PHYSICAL AND EMOTIONAL LEVEL, BUT ALSO ON A SOULFUL OR SPIRITUAL LEVEL.

OUR TWIN FLAMES ARE THE YING'S TO OUR YANG'S THE SUN TO OUR MOON, AND THE LIGHT TO OUR DARKNESS. TWIN FLAMES ARE ALSO OUR MIRRORS IN THAT THEY REFLECT TO US ALL OUR HIDDEN FEARS AND

SHADOWS, BUT ALSO OUR TRUE INNER BEAUTY AND STRENGTH. IN THIS WAY, OUR TWIN FLAMES OPEN THE DOOR TO TREMENDOUS EMOTIONAL, PSYCHOLOGICAL, AND SPIRITUAL GROWTH.

IN THE CURRENT DAY, WE ARE WITNESSING MORE AND MORE TWIN SOULS INCARNATING INTO THE PLANET AT THE SAME TIME TO COME TOGETHER FOR THE UNIFICATION AND ASCENSION PROCESS FOR THE BENEFIT OF ALL.

CHAPTER 13

THE PURPOSE OF TWIN FLAME RELATIONSHIPS

TWIN FLAMES ARE A DIVINE EXPRESSION OF BALANCE, HARMONY, AND UNCONDITIONAL LOVE. EVERY TWIN FLAME COUPLE WILL HAVE A HIGHER PURPOSE TO ACHIEVE TOGETHER, AND THIS MAY INCLUDE FROM RAISING CONSCIOUS CHILDREN AND STARTING AN ECO-CONSCIOUS BUSINESS, TO BECOMING SPIRITUAL GUIDES AND MENTORING THE LIVES OF OTHERS.

ACCORDING TO KELLEY ROSANO

ASTROLOGY TELLS US THE STORY ABOUT KARMA, PAST LIVES AND WHY

WE ARE ATTRACTED TO SPECIFIC PEOPLE. OUR PERSONAL PAST LIFE PATTERNS, PERSONALITIES AND BEHAVIOR ARE BEING ACTED OUT IN THE HERE AND NOW. IN OTHER WORDS, TIME IS AN ILLUSION. OUR PAST LIVES AND OUR FUTURE LIVES ARE RUNNING TOGETHER SIMULTANEOUSLY IN THE MOMENT.

THE GREATEST LOVE STORY EVER TOLD, IS THE ONE YOU HAVE WITH YOUR VERY OWN BELOVED TWIN FLAME. IN THE BEGINNING WE WERE CREATED IN GOD, ALPHA AND OMEGA IN AN OVOID WHITE FIRE SPIRIT LIGHT. GOD SPLIT THE SOUL INTO TWO IDENTICAL PARTS, TWIN FLAMES. EACH WITH THE SAME IDENTICAL SOUL BLUEPRINT. ONE CARRYING THE MALE POLARITY AND THE OTHER CARRYING THE FEMALE POLARITY.

THE TAI CHI IS THE SYMBOL FOR TWIN FLAMES. TWIN FLAMES AND LOVE SPIRALING IN INFINITY. WHEN 2 SOULS COME TOGETHER THAT ARE IDENTICAL AND CAN LOVE EACH OTHER IN A

LOVING AND HARMONIOUS WAY AND TURN THAT LOVE INTO A MISSION, IT CAN WIPE OUT ALL THE NEGATIVITY ON THE PLANET, BECAUSE THE POWER OF LOVE IS THE MOST POWERFUL FORCE IN ALL THE UNIVERSE AND WHEN TWIN FLAMES ARE UNITED IN LOVE, THAT LOVE ENERGY GOES OUT AND IT HEALS EVERYONE AND EVERYTHING.

SO, THE DARK FORCES DO WHATEVER THEY CAN TO PREVENT THESE TYPES OF UNIONS FROM OCCURRING. OFTEN, TWIN FLAMES DO NOT HAVE ENOUGH SELF-MASTERY TO MAINTAIN A HEALTHY RELATIONSHIP.

ROSANO CONTINUES BY SAYING YOU HAVE BEEN TRAINED TO EXPECT LOVE TO HURT, WHY WOULD THAT BE? WHY WOULD YOU HAVE TO HURT IN ORDER TO RECEIVE LOVE WHEN LOVE IS AVAILABLE FOR ALL, AT ALL TIMES? THE ROOT TO LOVE IS THROUGH THE HEART.

CHAPTER 14

WHAT IS A SOULMATE?

THE ARTICLE CONTINUES BY DESCRIBING THE DIFFERENCE BETWEEN SOULMATES AND TWIN SOULS. IT STATES AS FOLLOWS: "SOULMATES ARE OUR SOUL FAMILY, THE ONES WE DO HAVE MANY LIFETIMES AND EXPERIENCES WITH. THOSE WHO HELP US GROW AND EVOLVE, CREATE AND DISSIPATE KARMA."

IT CONTINUES BY STATING THAT ACCORDING TO ANCIENT WISDOM, WHEN THE SOUL IS "BORN" OR DESCENDED FROM THE SOURCE, IT IS CREATED IN A GROUP. THE SOULS OF THIS GROUP ARE OUR SOULMATES.

A SOULMATE IS SOMEONE YOU ARE CLOSE TO AT A SOUL LEVEL AND WITH WHOM YOU HAVE HAD MANY SHARED EXPERIENCES IN DIFFERENT LIFETIMES, IN VARIOUS KINDS OF RELATIONSHIPS---SIBLINGS, PARENT-CHILD, BEST FRIEND, AS WELL AS ROMANTIC RELATIONSHIPS.

THERE IS A DEEP LOVE FOR EACH OTHER, AND A SPIRITUAL BOND THAT SETS THEM APART FROM MOST OTHER PEOPLE IN YOUR LIFE. WE CAN HAVE MANY SOULMATES IN OUR LIVES, AND THEY COME TO US TO HELP US GROW SPIRITUALLY.

"LOVERS DON'T FINALLY MEET SOMEWHERE. THEY'RE IN EACH OTHER ALL ALONG."-RUMI (THE ESSENTIAL RUMI)

CHAPTER 15

THE DIVINE MASCULINE

In the weeks that followed, Rico found himself becoming more curious about this Twin Flame connection that Rhea had turned him on to. He couldn't help but admit to himself that the similarities in their relationship was definitely something to consider. He decided that more research was needed so that he would find out how or what his role in this connection would mean. How was he supposed to handle this situation? What was the end game to this Flame thing? As Rico began to delve deeper

INTO THE INFORMATION, HE FOUND THIS:

 ACCORDING TO MONICA LEONELLE GRACE

THERE ARE 14 TRAITS ASSOCIATED WITH A DIVINE MASCULINE LISTED AND IDENTIFIED IN AN ARTICLE TITLED "TRAITS OF THE DIVINE MASCULINE (AND HOW TO KNOW WHERE HE'S AT ON THE JOURNEY).

SHE LISTS THEM AS FOLLOWS:

RESPONSIBLE
VULNERABLE
ADVENTUROUS

COURAGEOUS

SOLUTIONS-ORIENTED

LOGICAL

PURSUANT

PROTECTIVE
GROUNDED
GIVING/PROVIDING
ACTION-ORIENTED
LEADING

BOUNDARY SETTER
STEADFAST

IN THIS ARTICLE, GRACE CONTINUES BY DEFINING THE ROLE OF THE DM.

RESPONSIBLE = THE DIVINE MASCULINE DOES NOT RUN FROM RESPONSIBILITY. HE SEES OPPORTUNITIES FOR RESPONSIBILITY AND READILY ACCEPTS THEM, HE EVEN LOOKS FOR WAYS TO EXPAND HIMSELF THROUGH TAKING ON NEW RESPONSIBILITIES.

AS THE DIVINE MASCULINE COMES INTO UNION WITH HIS DIVINE FEMININE, HE WILL FEEL RESPONSIBLE FOR HER IN MANY WAYS. HE WILL LOOK FOR WAYS TO TAKE ON MORE RESPONSIBILITY FOR HER WELL-BEING, HEALTH, SAFETY, FINANCES, AND GROWTH.

THIS DOES NOT MEAN HE WILL DO THINGS FOR HER UNNECESSARILY, AS THAT IS NOT GOING TO HELP HER GROW. RATHER, HE WILL INVEST IN HER GROWTH AND CREATE MORE ABUNDANCE FOR HIMSELF SO THAT HE HAS THE OVERFLOW TO TAKE ON THE RESPONSIBILITY OF CARING FOR HER.

VULNERABLE = THE DIVINE MASCULINE SHARES HIMSELF WITH HIS DIVINE FEMININE. NO TOPIC IS OFF LIMITS, AND HE IS ABLE TO SPEAK HIS TRUE MIND TO HER. WHILE HE DOESN'T ALWAYS FULLY UNDERSTAND HER THOUGHT PROCESS, HE STAYS OPEN TO HER WAY OF BEING AND APPRECIATES HER INSIGHT AND UNIQUE WAY OF LOOKING AT THE WORLD.

AS THE DIVINE MASCULINE MOVES TOWARD HIS FEMININE, HE WILL SHARE MORE AND MORE OF HIMSELF WITH HER. HE WILL READILY SPEAK TO HER ABOUT HIS CHALLENGES, PROBLEMS, AND FEARS. THIS DOES NOT MEAN THAT HE WILL TELL HER EVERYTHING, AND CERTAINLY NOT ON HER SCHEDULE. THE DIVINE MASCULINE IS MEANT TO LEAD THESE CONVERSATIONS. HE IS NOT EASILY MANIPULATED AND DOES NOT RETURN VULNERABILITY WITH MORE VULNERABILITY JUST FOR THE SAKE OF IT. HE INSTEAD, OFFERS

VULNERABILITY WHEN IT IS RIGHT FOR THE CONNECTION.

ADVENTUROUS = THE DIVINE MASCULINE COMES UP WITH LOTS OF FUN ADVENTURES FOR HIS DIVINE FEMININE AND FOR HIMSELF. HE EXPRESSES THROUGH ACTION AND IT'S TELLING WHEN HE HAS AN IDEA FOR THEM, BECAUSE IT SHOWS THAT HE HAS BEEN THINKING OF HER AND WANTS TO SPEND TIME WITH HER.

ADVENTURE IS SIMPLE, AND THE DIVINE MASCULINE LIKES TO DO SIMPLE THINGS WITH THE PEOPLE HE LOVES, INCLUDING HIS DIVINE FEMININE. HE TAKES PLEASURE IN SURPRISING HIS DIVINE FEMININE WITH NEW EXPERIENCES.

THIS DOES NOT NECESSARILY MEAN LAVISH MEALS, EXPENSIVE GIFTS, OR ROMANTIC TRIPS. ADVENTURE CAN MEAN SOMETHING DIFFERENT FOR EACH TWIN SOUL PAIRING. IT CAN MEAN ROAD TRIPS, TICKETS TO A PLAY OR MUSICAL, A NEW HOLE-IN-THE

WALL RESTAURANT, PLANTING A GARDEN, OR GYM MEMBERSHIPS. THE DIVINE FEMININE CAN DREAM OF THE ADVENTURES, AND THE DIVINE MASCULINE WILL MAKE IT HAPPEN FOR THE TWO OF THEM TOGETHER.

COURAGEOUS = THE DIVINE MASCULINE LEAVES BEHIND THE WINNER/LOSER PARADIGM AND TRADES IT FOR COURAGE. IT TAKES COURAGE TO PLAY THE GAME, ANY GAME. A GAME REQUIRES RISK, AND THE DIVINE MASCULINE MAY NOT WIN IN THE MATERIAL SENSE, BUT THE DIVINE MASCULINE KNOWS THAT HIS REAL BOUNTY IS THE GROWTH HE EXPERIENCES THROUGH THE TRYING. AS THE DIVINE MASCULINE MOVES THROUGH TOWARD HIS DIVINE FEMININE, HE WILL PLAY MORE GAMES AND AS A RESULT, ACCOMPLISH MORE IN LIFE. THOSE WHO PLAY RECEIVE WHAT THEY WANT MORE OFTEN, AND THE UNIVERSE LOVES PERSISTENCE ABOVE ALL.

THIS DOES NOT NECESSARILY MEAN THAT THE DIVINE MASCULINE WILL WIN GAMES ON BEHALF OF HIS DIVINE FEMININE. THIS IS A FEUDAL AND OUTDATED NOTION. HIS COURAGE IS NOT MEANT TO BE POURED INTO A "KNIGHT IN SHINING ARMOR" SCENARIO, AS THE DIVINE MASCULINE KNOWS AND ALWAYS HAS BELIEVED THAT THE DIVINE FEMININE CAN SAVE HERSELF.

MONICA CONTINUES HER DESCRIPTIONS OF THE DM'S TRAITS BY STATING THAT HE IS ALWAYS:

SOLUTIONS ORIENTED = THE DIVINE MASCULINE IS ORIENTED TOWARD SOLUTIONS. HE OBSERVES AND INTERACTS WITH THE WORLD THROUGH DESIRING TO SOLVE THE PROBLEMS IN IT. HE ALSO DESIRES TO SOLVE PROBLEMS FOR THE DIVINE FEMININE, ESPECIALLY WHEN THOSE PROBLEMS PLAY TO HIS NATURAL STRENGTHS, ABILITIES, AND SKILL SET.

THIS DOES NOT MEAN THAT THE DIVINE MASCULINE WILL SOLVE PROBLEMS THAT TAKE AWAY FROM THEIR DIVINE FEMININE'S GROWTH WORK. THIS IS AN IMPORTANT DISTINCTION! A DIVINE MASCULINE WILL NEVER TAKE A GROWTH OPPORTUNITY AWAY FROM A DIVINE FEMININE WHEN THAT GROWTH IS SOMETHING, SHE PERSONALLY DESIRES THAT WILL HELP HER REACH HER GOALS.

AT THE SAME TIME, NO PERSON CAN DO IT ALL BY THEMSELVES. THIS IS WHERE THE DIVINE MASCULINE WILL NATURALLY FILL IN THE GAPS AND THE DIVINE FEMININE DOES THE SAME FOR HIM ON HIS GROWTH JOURNEY.

LOGICAL = THE DIVINE MASCULINE USES LOGIC AND RATIONALITY TO GROUND DREAMS INTO REALITY. HE IS PRACTICAL AND FOCUSES ON SCHEDULES AND TASKS WITH EASE. HE LOVES PUTTING PLANS TO IDEAS AND EXCELS AT EXECUTION. AS HE MOVES TOWARDS HIS DIVINE FEMININE, HE'S ABLE TO TAKE HER

IDEAS AND PUT THEM INTO MOTION. HE OFFERS STRUCTURE, STABILITY, AND GUIDANCE FOR HOW TO MOVE THINGS FORWARD IN THE MATERIAL WORLD.

THIS DOES NOT MEAN THE DIVINE FEMININE HAS TO WAIT FOR HER MASCULINE TO COME AROUND IN ORDER TO START WORKING ON HER DREAMS. THE DIVINE FEMININE HAS THE DIVINE MASCULINE ENERGIES INSIDE HER AND CAN TAP INTO THEM AT ANY TIME TO MOVE HER OWN IDEAS FORWARD.

PURSUANT = THE DIVINE MASCULINE PURSUES HIS OWN LIFE. HE LEAVES BEHIND A DESIRE TO CONTROL OR INFLUENCE OTHER PEOPLE'S LIVES AND INSTEAD DEVELOPS HIS OWN INTERESTS, HOBBIES, AND GOALS. HE TRULY BELIEVES THAT LIFE IS A GIFT, AND HE IS COMFORTABLE IN HIS OWN SKIN, DOING HIS OWN THING.

AS HE MOVES TOWARD HIS DIVINE FEMININE, HE'S ALSO PURSUING

HER. THIS IS THE ULTIMATE DIVINE MASCULINE MOVE! HE KNOWS WHAT HE WANTS, AND HE GOES FOR IT WITH ALL HIS HEART. THIS DOES NOT MEAN THAT THE DIVINE FEMININE HAS TO WAIT ON HER DIVINE MASCULINE AS SHE CAN PURSUE HIM TOO! IT JUST MEANS WHEN THE MASCULINE IS COMFORTABLE GOING AFTER THE THINGS HE WANTS IN LIFE—WHEN HE HAS THE ENERGY AND IS WILLING TO EXERT IT TO CREATE A JUICY AND ZESTY EXPERIENCE FOR HIMSELF—THE FEMININE WILL KNOW IMMEDIATELY.

PROTECTIVE = THE DIVINE MASCULINE THROWS AWAY THE WEAKNESS/STRENGTH PARADIGM AND INSTEAD MOVES TOWARD A ROLE OF PROTECTOR OR GUARDIAN OVER THE ONES HE LOVES. HE NOTICES INJUSTICE AND WORKS HARD TO BALANCE ALL UNFAIRNESS HE SEES. HE ACCUMULATES STRENGTH NOT TO MAKE A GRAB A POWER, *BUT RATHER SO THAT HIS CUP OVERFLOWS AND HE'S ABLE TO PROTECT* HIMSELF AND THOSE AROUND HIM.

THE DIVINE MASCULINE'S PROTECTIVENESS EXTENDS BEYOND HIS DIVINE FEMININE AND TO OTHERS AS WELL, INCLUDING CHILDREN, ANIMALS, AND OTHER DIVINE MASCULINES. THE DIVINE MASCULINE IS NOT TRYING TO DOMINATE OTHER DIVINE MASCULINES OR COMPETE WITH THEM, BUT RATHER, EXTEND THE PROTECTION HE'S ABLE TO OFFER TO ALL OTHER BEINGS.

THIS DOES NOT MEAN THE DIVINE MASCULINE GOES OVERBOARD IN TRYING TO PROTECT HIS FEMININE. THIS IS TO BE PRESENT AND ORIENTED NOT ABOUT HIM BEING JEALOUS OR ATTEMPTING TO KEEP OTHER MASCULINES AWAY FROM HER. RATHER, THE DIVINE SPIRITUALLY, HE IS ABLE TO ENERGETICALLY CONNECT WITH THE EARTH'S CORE WHICH ALLOWS HIM TO BE PRESENT AND ORIENTED WITHIN THE STRUCTURE OF THE MATERIAL WORLD. MASCULINE IS FULLY AWARE OF HIS CAPABILITIES AS WELL AS HIS LACK OF CONTROL OVER WHAT HAPPENS TO OTHER BEINGS

THAT HE LOVES AND CARES ABOUT. HE DOES NOT OVEREXTEND HIMSELF IN TRYING TO PROTECT OTHERS AND HAS REALISTIC EXPECTATIONS AROUND IT.

GROUNDED = THE DIVINE MASCULINE IS GROUNDED, SENSIBLE, AND WISE. BECAUSE OF HIS NATURAL ORIENTATION TOWARD THE PHYSICAL WORLD, HE TENDS TO MAKE LOGICAL, RATIONAL, AND "GOOD" DECISIONS.

AS THE DIVINE MASCULINE INTERACTS WITH HIS DIVINE FEMININE, HE IS ABLE TO GROUND HER SPIRITUAL CONNECTION INTO THE MATERIAL WORLD. HE HELPS HER STAY CONNECTED TO HER 3D REALITY AROUND HER AND HELPS THE MANIFESTATIONS SHE CREATES SHE CREATES COME ALIVE ON EARTH. HE ALSO MOVES EXCESS ENERGY FROM THE CONNECTION INTO THE EARTH, WHICH CAN ABSORB LIMITLESS AMOUNTS OF ENERGY THAT THE TWO PHYSICAL BODIES IN THE UNION CAN'T HOLD.

THIS DOES NOT MEAN THAT THE DIVINE MASCULINE IS ALWAYS GROUNDED OR THAT THE DIVINE FEMININE IS ALWAYS UP IN THE CLOUDS. IT SIMPLY MEANS THE TWO COUNTERPARTS NATURALLY GRAVITATE (AND WERE MADE FOR) DIFFERENT PURPOSES.

GIVING = THE DIVINE MASCULINE WAS DESIGNED TO GIVE AND PROVIDE. IT IS THE ENERGY OF ACCUMULATING MATERIAL RESOURCES TO THOSE HE FEELS RESPONSIBILITY FOR.

WHEN THE DIVINE MASCULINE AND DIVINE FEMININE COME INTO UNION, THEY WILL TAKE ON THESE NATURAL ROLES OF GIVING (THE MASCULINE) AND RECEIVING (THE FEMININE).

THIS IS CHALLENGING IN TODAY'S SOCIETY AND REQUIRES BOTH COUNTERPARTS TO CHECK THEIR EGOS AT THE DOOR. THE MASCULINES, PROVIDE TO THE FEMININES AND THE FEMININE RECEIVES IN ORDER TO DO WHAT SHE DOES BEST TO CONNECT TO THE SPIRITUAL, RECEIVE INTUITIVE

INFORMATION AND MESSAGES, NURTURE HER DIVINE MASCULINE AND ANY CHILDREN, FAMILY, OR FRIENDS THEY HAVE, AND MORE.

THIS DOES NOT MEAN THAT THE DIVINE MASCULINE MUST BE THE BREADWINNER, OR THAT THE DIVINE FEMININE CANNOT BE SUCCESSFUL AND MAKE GOOD MONEY AND PROVIDE AS WELL. THIS IS ABOUT ENERGY!

ACTION-ORIENTED = THE DIVINE MASCULINE TAKES ACTION. UNLIKE THE DIVINE FEMININE, WHO IS RECEPTIVE AND ATTRACTS RESOURCES TO HER, THE DIVINE MASCULINE GOES OUT AND GATHERS RESOURCES. AS THE DIVINE MASCULINE MOVES TOWARD HIS DIVINE FEMININE, HE'LL MOVE FROM HERMIT ENERGY, WHERE HE DISENGAGES OR PULLS BACK TO PROTECT HIS ENERGY, INTO A FLURRY OF ACTION. AT FIRST, THIS ACTION MAY OR MAY NOT INCLUDE HIS DIVINE FEMININE, BUT AS THEIR RELATIONSHIP GROWS DEEPER INTO UNION, THESE ACTIONS WILL MORE

FREQUENTLY INVOLVE PLANS AND TIME WITH HIS DIVINE FEMININE.

THIS DOES NOT MEAN HE WILL DO EVERYTHING FOR THE DIVINE FEMININE, OR THAT SHE GETS TO SIT AROUND WHILE HE DOES ALL THE WORK. BOTH COUNTERPARTS DO DEEP WORK, NEITHER OF WHICH IS ELEVATED ABOVE THE OTHER.

LEADING = THE DIVINE MASCULINE IS A LEADER WITH HIS DIVINE FEMININE AND WITHIN HIS COMMUNITY. HE DOES NOT LEAD BY ACCUMULATING POWER OR CONTROL, BUT RATHER LEADS FROM A PLACE OF LOVE AND SECURITY.

THE DIVINE MASCULINE DOESN'T SEE LEADERSHIP AS A HIERARCHY. HE DOES NOT TRY TO DOMINATE OTHER DIVINE MASCULINE'S AROUND HIM OR COMPETE WITH THEM FOR A PLACE AT THE TOP OF THE MOUNTAIN. RATHER, HE BELIEVES IN THE ABILITY OF EVERYONE TO BE A LEADER WITHIN THEIR NATURAL STRENGTHS AND

TALENTS AND CHECKS HIS EGO AT THE DOOR.

HE SEES HIS POSITION AS A LEADER TO HELP GROW AND STRENGTHEN OTHERS IN LEADING AND TAKES ON THE ROLE OF TEACHING OR MENTORING HIS PEOPLE. HE INVESTS IN HIS PEOPLE AND HELP BUILDS THEM UP. AS HE GROWS CLOSER TO HIS DIVINE FEMININE, SHE MAY SEE HIS LEADERSHIP SKILLS IMPROVE AT WORK OR WITHIN THEIR SOCIAL CIRCLE. SHE WILL ALSO SEE HIS LEADERSHIP IN THE WAYS THAT HE TAKES INITIATIVE IN BUILDING THEIR LIVES TOGETHER.

HE DOES NOT MEAN THAT THE DIVINE FEMININE ISN'T ALSO A LEADER, BECAUSE SHE IS! THE TWO LEADS IN VERY DIFFERENT WAYS. THE DIVINE FEMININE LEADS FROM A PLACE OF FLOW, CREATIVITY, AND INTUITION, WHILE THE DIVINE MASCULINE LEADS FROM A PLACE OF STRUCTURE, STABILITY, AND ACTION.

BOUNDARY SETTER = THE DIVINE MASCULINE SETS BOUNDARIES WITH NOT ONLY DIVINE FEMININE, BUT EVERYONE ELSE AS WELL. HE LEAVES BEHIND THE NOTION OF RULES AND ORDER AND REALIZES THAT HE CANNOT CONTROL THE ACTIONS OF OTHERS, BUT HE CAN CHOOSE HOW HE RESPONDS TO THEM—AND THE WAY HE RESPONDS TO THEM IS BY SETTING BOUNDARIES WITH OTHERS.

BOUNDARIES ARE BASED ON A LOGIC TREE. EACH POSSIBLE SCENARIO HAS A BRANCH, AND THE DIVINE MASCULINE EXCELS AT FIGURING OUT HOW HE IS GOING TO RESPOND TO EACH OF THE BRANCHES. HE DOES THIS BY SETTING BOUNDARIES AND COMMUNICATING THEM TO ALL INTERESTED AND INVOLVED PARTIES.

A FULLY EMBODIED DIVINE MASCULINE WILL ALWAYS COMMUNICATE HIS BOUNDARIES IN WORDS. DIVINE MASCULINE'S WHO ARE STILL HEALING AND WORKING ON THEMSELVES MAY COMMUNICATE THEIR BOUNDARIES

THROUGH OTHER METHODS OF NONVERBAL COMMUNICATION. THIS IS NOT IDEAL TO THOSE AROUND THEM, BUT THEY ARE STILL MOVING IN THE RIGHT DIRECTION BY SETTING THOSE BOUNDARIES TO BEGIN WITH.

STEADFAST = THE DIVINE MASCULINE IS SECURE AND STABLE IN BOTH HIS LOVE AND AFFECTION FOR HIS FEMININE AND IN OTHER MAJOR AREAS OF HIS LIFE. HE HELPS OTHERS AROUND HIM FEEL SECURE BY BEING THERE FOR THEM WHEN THEY'RE IN NEED.

LIKE A FURNACE IN WINTER THAT KEEPS THE FAMILY WARM, THE DIVINE MASCULINE PROVIDES A DEEP SENSE OF HOME AND SECURITY AS HE MOVES TOWARD HIS FEMININE. AS A RESULT, SHE IS ABLE TO MAINTAIN HER FAITH IN THE CONNECTION AND BUILD A STRONG BRIDGE BETWEEN THEIR UNION AND THEIR HIGHER POWER.

THE DIVINE MASCULINE UNDERSTANDS HIS ROLE IN THE UNION. HE PROVIDES

SAFETY, SECURITY, AND STABILITY AND HIS FEMININE IS ABLE TO RETURN THAT TO HIM. AS THEY GROW TOWARD EACH OTHER, THEY GROW TOWARD THEIR HIGHER POWER AS WELL. ALL EITHER COUNTERPART MUST DO IS MAKE THE OTHER FEEL SECURE TO REAP THESE BENEFITS.

CHAPTER 16

A POWERFUL EXPLOSION/THE KUNDALINI AWAKENING

RHEA WAS EXCITED THAT RICO ASKED HER TO PLAN THEIR NEXT DATE NIGHT AND JUST LET HIM KNOW THE WHERE AND WHEN. IT JUST HAPPENED THAT SHE HAD BEEN WAITING TO SHOW OFF SOME LINGERIE AND OTHER GOODIES SHE HAD PURCHASED BEFORE THEY SO ABRUPTLY WENT THEIR SEPARATE WAYS LAST FALL. NOW, SHE HAD THE CHANCE TO SHOW RICO JUST EXACTLY WHAT HE'D BEEN MISSING, AND SHE INTENDED TO GIVE HIM A NIGHT HE WOULD REMEMBER FOR A VERY LONG TIME.

SHE BOUGHT HIS FAVORITE MIXED DRINKS AND PLACED THEM IN THE COOLER TO CHILL WHILE SHE ORDERED THEIR MEAL INSTEAD OF COOKING IT SO SHE WOULDN'T BE TIRED AND OVERWHELMED FROM COOKING. SHE TURNED ON HER FAVORITE MIXED CD AND TOOK A LONG RELAXING BUBBLE BATH BEFORE HER FOOD ORDER ARRIVED.

RHEA PUT ON HER RED FUZZY MULE SLIPPERS FROM FREDERICKS OF HOLLYWOOD WHICH WAS HER FAVORITE LINGERIE BOUTIQUE. SHE PUT HER HAIR IN A CUTESY UP-DUE STYLE AND PUT ON HER NEW SHORT BABY DOLL LINGERIE SET WITH THE RUFFLED RED PANTIES THAT MATCHED. SHE TOOK ESPECIALLY EXTRA CARE WITH HER MAKE-UP MAKING SURE SHE WORE THE RED SHINY LIPSTICK THAT HE LOVED TO SEE ON HER FULL SENSUOUS LIPS.

ONE LAST CHECK IN THE MIRROR TO MAKE SURE EVERYTHING WAS ON POINT BEFORE SHE LEFT TO OPEN

THE DOOR FOR THE DELIVERY FOOD SERVICE GUY. RHEA TOSSED ON HER MATCHING ROBE TO COMPLETE THE LINGERIE ASSEMBLE AND TO MAKE ABSOLUTE SURE EVERYTHING WAS HIDDEN UNDERNEATH FROM THE DELIVERY GUY'S PRYING EYES BEFORE SHE OPENED THE DOOR.

SHE REALLY LOVED THE CLASSY STYLES OF FREDERICK'S LINGERIE LINE BECAUSE IT HAD INTRODUCED A SPECIALTY LINE OF BRAS AND MATCHING PANTIES THAT OTHER SHOPS DIDN'T HAVE FOR WOMEN WHO WERE AMPLY ENDOWED IN THE TOP AREA. SHE COULD HAVE KISSED THE PERSON WHO THOUGHT OF THESE BEAUTIFUL PATTERNS AND LACY SEXY SETS THAT FIT HER WELL AND SHOWED OFF HER MOST VOLUPTUOUS ASSETS. NOW TO MAKE AN UNFORGETTABLE IMPRESSION ON HER MAN.

RICO RANG THE DOORBELL TO RHEA'S HOUSE RIGHT ON TIME. HE COULDN'T HELP BUT BE A LITTLE CURIOUS ABOUT THE PLANS SHE'D MADE FOR

THE EVENING. HE KNEW IT WOULD BE SOMETHING WONDERFUL BECAUSE SHE ALWAYS MADE THEIR DATES FUN AND EXCITING. RICO COULD HEAR BEAUTIFUL MUSIC COUPLED WITH DELICIOUS SMELLS OF SOMETHING COMING FROM THE KITCHEN WAFTING THROUGH THE DOOR AS RHEA OPENED IT. RIGHT AWAY HE NOTICED HOW SHE LOOKED LIKE A MILLION DOLLARS IN THE GLAMOROUS LINGERIE OUTFIT.

RHEA GAVE HER MAN A SENSUOUS SMILE THAT LIT UP HER EYES AND HIS HEART. WHOA , HE WHISPERED TO HIMSELF AS HIS HEART BEGAN TO BEAT HARDER AND FASTER. RICO WATCHED THAT SEXY ASS OF HERS SASHAY ACROSS THE ROOM DURING WHAT SHE CALLED A WALK IN FRONT OF HIM. HE LOOKED AWAY QUICKLY BEFORE THE BUMP IN HIS PANTS BECAME EVEN BIGGER AND NOTICEABLE.

WOW, HE THOUGHT, AS HE SAW THE SPREAD SHE HAD LAID OUT FOR THEM WITH CANDLELIGHT AND HIS FAVORITE

DRINKS AND DESSERT. SHE HAD A FEW SMALL ROUND CROCKS WITH PEACH COBBLER INSIDE WHICH SHE KNEW WERE HIS FAVORITE DESSERT. THIS WOULD MOST DEFINITELY BE A NIGHT TO REMEMBER HE THOUGHT. HE COULD ALREADY FEEL IT IN HIS BONES.

RHEA HAD SET THE BEDROOM UP EARLIER WITH AROMA THERAPY CANDLES, HIMALAYAN SALT LAMPS THAT GAVE OFF A NICE COLORED GLOW AND BROUGHT AN EXOTIC FEEL TO THE ROOM. SHE HAD A MASSAGE TABLE SET UP IN THE LARGE BEDROOM WITH MASSAGE OIL, TOWELS, AND OTHER EQUIPMENT THAT WOULD AID IN THE INTERESTING NIGHT SHE HAD PLANNED FOR THE LOVERS.

THE TWO TOOK THEIR TIME WITH DINNER SAVING DESSERT UNTIL LATER. THEY PLAYED MUSIC, SANG OLDIES TOGETHER, FAST DANCED AND SLOW DANCED AS THEY BOTH ALLOWED THE DELICIOUS MEAL TO DIGEST IN THEIR TUMMIES. THEY CAME

TOGETHER ON THE LAST SLOW DANCE THAT DREW THEM DEEPER INTO EACH OTHER'S ARMS AND DEEPER STILL AGAINST EACH OTHER'S BODY.

THEY DANCED AND PRESSED INTO EACH OTHER KISSING AND STRIPPING OFF TOP LAYERS OF CLOTHING AS THEY BACKED ALL THE WAY INTO THE BEDROOM. AT FIRST, RICO DIDN'T SEE THE MASSAGE TABLE AND OTHER GOODIES THAT ACCOMPANIED IT UNTIL RHEA STOPPED HIM COLD AND WHISPERED SOFTLY "OPEN YOUR EYES BABY, NOW LAY FACE DOWN ON THE TABLE."

RICO POLITELY DID AS HE WAS TOLD AND ALLOWED HIS LADY LOVE TO UNDRESS HIM THE REST OF THE WAY UNTIL HE LAY STRETCHED OUT IN HIS BIRTHDAY SUIT WEARING NOTHING BUT A SMILE. JESUS THIS WOMAN COULD GET HIM OVERHEATED HE THOUGHT AS HE TRIED TO ADJUST HIMSELF TO A COMFORTABLE POSITION FACE DOWN ON THE TABLE. WHAT HAD

SHE PLANNED FOR THE REST OF HIS EVENING?

RHEA GENTLY AND SLOWLY POURED WARM MASSAGING OIL OVER HIS BODY. SHE WORKED THE OIL IN MAKING SLOW MASSAGING CIRCLES FROM FRONT TO BACK THEN FRONT AGAIN MAKING SURE TO BE GENTLE WITH HIS FULL TESTICLES WHILE RUNNING HER SMALL FINGERTIPS UP AND DOWN AND IN AND OUT OF HIS NICE FIRM BUTTOCKS.

SHE COULD HEAR HIS MOANS BECOME A LITTLE LOUDER AND HIS BREATHING BECOME SHALLOWER. RHEA KNEW INSTINCTIVELY THAT SHE WAS PLEASURING HER MAN AS HE HAD DONE SO MANY TIMES IN THE PAST TO HER. SUDDENLY AND WITHOUT WARNING, RICO TURNED OVER SHOWING FULL FRONTAL NUDITY WHICH MADE HER TAKE A DEEP BREATH. NO MATTER HOW MANY TIMES SHE'D SEEN THIS MAN'S BODY, SHE STILL BECAME HOT AND

FLUSTERED AT THE SIGHT OF IT DRESSED OR UNDRESSED.

SHE REACHED OUT HER HANDS AGAIN TO MASSAGE HIS FRONT THIS TIME BUT WAS ABRUPTLY INTERRUPTED BY RICO PULLING HER DOWN ON TOP OF HIM AND UNDRESSING HER ALL AT THE SAME TIME. HE UNSNAPPED THE LACY LINGERIE WITH EXPERTISE LEAVING HER BODY AS EXPOSED AS HIS WAS. RHEA GRABBED HIS ARM AND PULLED AT HIM INDICATING IT WAS TIME TO MOVE TOWARDS THE BED. AS HE GOT TO HIS FEET, RICO CAUGHT RHEA AROUND HER WAIST AND PROPELLED HER SOFT SUPPLE BODY TOWARDS THE BED.

RICO PLACED HER ON THE BED WITH A LESS THAN GENTLE THUD WHICH MADE HER WONDER IF HE WERE ANGRY ABOUT SOMETHING. HER QUESTIONS WERE ANSWERED NOT LONG AFTER SHE WONDERED ABOUT THEM AS SHE IMMEDIATELY BECAME HIS PREY FOR THE NIGHT. THE LOOK IN RICO'S EYES SHOWED SHEAR ANIMALISTIC

HUNGER. A PASSION FOR HER THAT MADE HER REALIZE THAT SHE WAS NO MATCH FOR THE KIND OF LOVEMAKING HE WAS DISPLAYING. AT THAT POINT, SHE KNEW ALL SHE COULD DO WAS SUBMIT TO HIS SAVAGE LOVEMAKING TECHNIQUE AND HOLD ON FOR DEAR LIFE.

HE PINNED HER HANDS ABOVE HER HEAD WITH ONE HAND AND POSITIONED HIMSELF ABOVE HER WITH THE OTHER. RICO THEN BEGAN THE RITUAL OF MAKING SLOW THEN FAST PASSIONATE LOVE TO HER REPEATEDLY. RHEA HAD NO CHOICE BUT TO SUBMIT TO HIS SKILLFUL LOVEMAKING. LOVEMAKING THAT LEFT HER SO FULL OF SUCH PLEASURE SHE THOUGHT SHE'D NEARLY GO MAD!

RICO CONTINUED HIS LOVEMAKING RITUAL AS HIS BODY MOVED LIKE A MACHINE THAT KNEW NO BOUNDARIES OR END.

ALL HE KNEW WAS HE FELT LIKE A ROCKET THAT HAD BEEN BLASTED

INTO SOMEWHERE THAT HAD NO TIME OR SPACE OR ANYTHING LESS THAN PURE UNADULTERATED HOT, WET, SOFT, JUICY, WOMANLY FLESH LIKE NOTHING HE'D EVER FELT IN HIS LIFE BEFORE AND HE WOULDN'T STOP, COULDN'T STOP IF HE TRIED. RICO BEGAN TO MAKE HARD, DEEP, PASSIONATE LOVE TO RHEA AS FAST AS HE COULD FOR WHAT SEEMED LIKE HOURS. SUDDENLY, HE FELT RHEA BEGAN TO SHAKE ALL OVER. HE LEANED OVER AND ASKED IF SHE WERE ALRIGHT AND COULD SEE HER NOD YES, BUT NO WORDS CAME OUT.

FOR THE FIRST TIME DURING THEIR LOVEMAKING, RHEA GRABBED A HOLD OF RICO'S STRONG ARMS AND SCREAMED LOUDLY AS SHE ALMOST COLLAPSED FROM THE IMMENSE PLEASURE.

AFTER BOTH COMPLETED THE SOUL STIRRING JOURNEY, BOTH RICO AND RHEA CONTINUED TO HOLD ON TO EACH OTHER FOR DEAR LIFE, AGAIN

WONDERING WHAT IN THE HELL HAD JUST HAPPENED TO THEM?

RICO COULD STILL FEEL RHEA'S BODY SHAKING AND TREMBLING AS IF SHE WAS IN AN EARTHQUAKE. HE GENTLY LAID HER DOWN ON THE BED AND TOLD HER TO STAY THERE. HE LEANED ON THE TALL CHEST DRESSER TRYING TO CATCH HIS BREATH AND WILL HIS HEARTRATE TO BECOME SLOW AND STEADY BECAUSE IT WAS POUNDING HARD AND FAST IN HIS CHEST.

RICO BEGAN TO THINK, AT THAT, MOMENT, AFTER HE GOT HIS BEARINGS AND HEADED FOR THE RESTROOM THAT THIS WAS NO ORDINARY SITUATION. HE KNEW THAT SOMETHING MAGICAL HAD TRANSPIRED BETWEEN HIM AND HIS WOMAN AND NO ONE COULD EVER CONVINCE HIM THAT THIS WAS ANYTHING LIKE A NORMAL LOVEMAKING SESSION.

RICO FELT AS IF HIS WHOLE BODY HAD BEEN TAKEN OVER BY SOME STRANGE

ENTITY AND HE HAD NO POWER OF HIS OWN TO SPEAK OF.

HE COULD NOT EXPLAIN ANY OF THIS AND DIDN'T EVEN KNOW HOW OR WHOM HE COULD HAVE TALKED TO ABOUT IT. WHO WOULD EVEN BELIEVE HIM IF HE FOUND THE RIGHT WORDS TO TRY AND EXPLAIN WHAT HE HIMSELF DIDN'T UNDERSTAND? HE FINALLY GOT UP ENOUGH NERVE TO ADMIT TO HIMSELF THAT FOR THE FIRST TIME IN HIS LIFE HE WAS AFRAID TO TOUCH A WOMAN AGAIN.

CHAPTER 17

THE AWAKENING OF THE KUNDALINI CONTINUED

RHEA STAYED LYING IN THE SAME POSITION RICO HAD PLACED HER IN FOR SEVERAL HOURS. SHE WAS STILL SHAKING SLIGHTLY BUT FINALLY BECAME ABLE TO GET TO HER FEET AND MOVE TOWARD THE SHOWER. SHE KEPT PLAYING AND RE-PLAYING OVER IN HER HEAD WHAT HAD TRANSPIRED BETWEEN HER AND RICO. NOTHING SHE CAME UP WITH COULD EXPLAIN WHAT HAD TAKEN PLACE ON THAT NIGHT. RHEA RECALLED THE LOOK ON RICO'S FACE AS SHE SHAKILY GOT HERSELF INTO THE SHOWER.

She desperately needed to feel the touch of hot water on her body to know this night was indeed reality and not something dragged into their lives from the Twilight Zone.

None of it made any sense. The look in Rico's eyes had made her feel a bit uneasy as he seemed to be in some kind of trance, or under some type of spell. He definitely acted different from the man she had grown accustomed to.

Rhea let the hot soothing water wash over her body, but nothing could erase this night from her mind. Nor did she want it too. She realized that this man had full, total, and complete control of her body and she'd never felt so much like a woman, all woman, under his touch in her life.

It felt scary good and magical and unbelievable all rolled into

ONE. BUT EVEN WITH THE REALIZATION THAT SOMETHING MAGICAL HAD INDEED HAPPENED TO THE LOVERS, SHE KNEW INSTINCTIVELY THAT THIS WASN'T ANYTHING ORDINARY AND SHE HAD TO FIND OUT WHAT HAPPENED HERE BEFORE SHE LEFT THIS EARTH.

RHEA BEGAN EXPLORING THE TWIN FLAME CONNECTION AGAIN AND THIS TIME SHE GOT MORE UNEXPECTED ANSWERS. SHE KNEW THAT WHAT SHE FOUND WAS THE MOST ACCURATE EXPLANATION THERE WAS FOR WHAT OCCURRED BETWEEN THEM THAT NIGHT.

RHEA FOUND SOMETHING REMARKABLY INTERESTING THAT DAY AND SHE KNEW THAT WHAT OCCURRED BETWEEN HER AND HER MAN THE LAST TIME THEY WERE INTIMATE, HAD PROBABLY CHANGED THEM FOREVER. SHE COULD NOT HAVE KNOWN HOW TRUE THOSE THOUGHTS WERE UNTIL SHE DISCOVERED THE AWAKENING OF THE KUNDALINI DURING SEX HAD INDEED BEEN THE GAME CHANGER!

Rhea read many articles that day explaining the meaning of the awakening of the kundalini. She was both shocked and intrigued by what she found because even though she'd been an avid reader all her life, this territory was new to her.

The first article was by a gentleman named Aleksandra Pesic titled Kundalini awakening and the first chakra-sexuality and fear.

Mr. Pesic described this phenomenon as follows:

The awakening of the Kundalini Shakti is as much an energetic, as it is a physical phenomenon. When the conditions necessary for awakening align—Boom comes an explosion in your body! From that moment on, you begin to see the world with different eyes. Everything's the same, yet everything's changed.

ALL OF A SUDDEN, YOUR BELIEFS ARE CONFIRMED, AND YOU HAVE BECOME AWARE OF THE EXISTENCE OF ENERGETIC BODIES. YOU FEEL ENERGY ALL AROUND YOU AND NOW YOU REALIZE THAT THERE IS A WORLD BEYOND THE FIVE SENSES. ENERGETIC SENSATIONS ARE SPREADING ALL OVER YOUR BODY, YOU CAN FEEL THE VIBRATIONS, THE TINGLING, THE ITCHING CRAWLING UP AND DOWN, THE SHIFTING OF HOT AND COLD WAVES, YOUR BODY IS SWEATING AND SHUDDERING. YOUR HEAD IS PULSATING, THERE IS A LUMP IN YOUR THROAT, YOU FEEL AS IF YOUR HANDS ARE RADIATING ENERGY, ELECTRIC SHOCKS ARE SHAKING YOU, YOUR BODY STARTS DANCING OUTSIDE YOUR CONTROL, THERE IS A WHISTLE IN YOUR EAR, YOU ARE HAVING VISIONS, DREAMS ARE MORE VIVID OR THEY DISAPPEAR ALTOGETHER, YOUR METABOLISM IS CHANGING, YOUR HABITS AND WISHES ARE CHANGING. THERE ARE INNUMERABLE, DIFFERENT SYMPTOMS FOLLOWING AWAKENING, THROUGH

WHICH THE BODY IS ADAPTING TO THE NEWBORN ENERGY....

PESIC CONTINUES TO TALK ABOUT THE ENERGY THAT, THE AWAKENING OF THE KUNDALINI BRINGS IN HIS ARTICLE, BUT RHEA FOUND THAT THE EXPLANATION HE HAD GIVEN HAD BEST DESCRIBED HER EXPERIENCE IN EXACT DETAIL AND SOMEHOW, SHE KNEW WITHOUT A DOUBT THAT THIS WAS INDEED WHAT HAD TRANSPIRED BETWEEN HER AND RICO. SHE WOULD SHARE THIS ARTICLE WITH HIM THE NEXT TIME THEY SPOKE SO THAT HE TOO WOULD BE ENLIGHTENED AND TOGETHER THEY COULD FIGURE OUT WHAT TO DO ABOUT INTIMACY AFTER THIS.

RHEA CONTINUED TO READ SEVERAL ARTICLES ON THE AWAKENING OF THE KUNDALINI, BUT SHE WAS MOST INTERESTED IN THE INFORMATION OFFERED THAT REFERRED TO THE TWIN FLAME CONNECTION AND THE KUNDALINI AWAKENING WHICH SHE

REALIZED NOW WAS WHAT SHE AND RICO HAD EXPERIENCED.

RHEA FOUND THE NEXT ARTICLE WRITTEN BY AN UNKNOWN AUTHOR THAT REFERRED TO A SOCIAL MEDIA POST AT THE END. THE ARTICLE SIMPLY STATED THAT "KUNDALINI AWAKENING NATURALLY OCCURS WHEN TWIN FLAMES ENGAGE IN SEXUAL INTIMACY, MOST PEOPLE WILL GO THROUGH LIFE WITH THEIR KUNDALINI ENERGY REMAINING DORMANT, THIS AWAKENING IS PART OF THE GIFT GIVEN TO TWIN FLAMES… IT BECOMES A PHYSICAL, ENERGETIC (LOVE ENERGY), EMOTIONAL AND SPIRITUAL EXCHANGE.

AS RHEA READ ARTICLE UPON ARTICLE ABOUT THE TWIN FLAME SEXUAL EXPERIENCE, SHE BEGAN TO UNDERSTAND IN DEPT THAT WHEN TWIN FLAMES COME TOGETHER IN INTIMACY, IF THEY ARE TRUE TWIN FLAMES THAT HAVE BEEN DIVINELY DESTINED AND GUIDED BY GOD, THEY WILL HAVE BEEN GIFTED A GIFT SO

RARE AND PRECIOUS THAT NO ONE AND NOTHING WOULD BE ABLE TO STOP ITS MAGIC.

THE TWIN'S SEXUAL UNION IS NOT ONE THAT IS MERELY PHYSICAL, BUT IS A SEXUAL UNION WITH THE SPIRIT, AND SOUL AS WELL AS THE BODY! THEY WILL HAVE EXPERIENCED SOMETHING MOST PEOPLE NEVER DREAM OF WHICH WAS CREATED BY THE ALMIGHTY HIMSELF FOR THE ULTIMATE PLEASURE OF THE TWO TO SHARE, AND WHILE THEY ARE JOINED, THEY ARE ONE SOUL, ONE SPIRIT, ONE BODY WHICH WAS THEIR DIVINE PURPOSE FOR BEING ON EARTH UNTIL THEIR FINAL ASCENSION IN THE FIRST PLACE.

THE INTENSITY OF THE SEXUAL UNION BETWEEN THE TWO WAS DESIGNED SO THAT NEITHER TWIN WOULD HAVE ANY DOUBT AS TO WHOM THEIR OTHER HALF WAS, AND TO RECOGNIZE THAT IF THE SEXUAL EXPERIENCE WERE ANY MORE INTENSE, NO HUMAN WOULD OR COULD SURVIVE IT. RHEA NOW

KNEW FOR SURE, THAT SHE AND HER BELOVED'S KUNDALINI WAS INDEED NOW AWAKENED, AND ONLY GOD COULD HELP THEM DOWN THE PATH OF THIS DIVINE UNION NOW.

CHAPTER 18

TRAITS OF THE DIVINE FEMININE

According to the article by Divine Feminine Alchemy August 2019

There are 7 listed Traits of the Divine Feminine which are:

1. Creativity = The Divine Feminine is the creative force that brings all things into existence...

2. Warrior Spirit...

3. Deep Sense of Justice, Balance, and Morality...

4. PASSIVE RESISTANCE...

5. STRONGER AWARENESS OF THOUGHTS AND FEELINGS...

6. HAVING A MANY-SIDED PERSONALITY...

7. FEELING THE NEED TO SELF-SACRIFICE TO REMAIN VIRTUOUS...

AUGUST 26, 2019 ARTICLE TITLED 7 CHARACTERISTICS OF FEMININE ENERGY

FEMININE ENERGY, MODERN WOMAN STATES THAT:

"THE DIVINE FEMININE ENERGY DISPLAYS ITSELF IN MANY FORMS, ACROSS MANY SPECIES. THERE ARE 7 CHARACTERISTICS OF FEMININE ENERGY...

1. *CREATIVITY* = THE DIVINE FEMININE IS THE CREATIVE FORCE THAT BRINGS ALL THINGS INTO EXISTENCE. THE BEST

PLACE TO SEE THIS IN ACTION IS IN NATURE. WE CAN CLEARLY SEE THE MANIFESTATION OF THE DIVINE FEMININE IN THE PROCESS OF PROCREATION.

THE FEMININE IS THE ONLY PRINCIPLE IN EXISTENCE WITH THE ABILITY TO TAKE IN SOMETHING AND TRANSMUTE IT INTO SOMETHING ELSE.

THE FEMALE BODY CAN TAKE A SEED, PLANT IT FOR APPROXIMATELY NINE MONTHS, AND TURN IT INTO AN ENTIRE VEHICLE TO HOUSE A CONSCIOUS BEING FOR 70+YEARS.

THERE IS A CERTAIN MAJESTIC QUALITY ABOUT A WOMAN THAT CANNOT BE DEFINED BY LOGIC OR SEMANTICS. THIS QUALITY THAT MAKES YOU FEEL CURIOUS, VULNERABLE,

AND ENCHANTED IS THE DIVINE FEMININE ENERGY. ON A MICRO LEVEL, IT IS WHY YOU CAN HAVE A HORRIBLE DAY AND BE INSTANTLY CHEERED UP BY A HUG FROM YOUR MOM.

ON A MACRO LEVEL, IT IS WHAT RAISES A MAN'S KUNDALINI SO HE MAY COMPOUND THE RESOURCES HE ACQUIRES WITH HIS PROTECTOR/ SURVIVOR NATURE AND BUILD A KINGDOM TO PROVIDE FOR 100 PEOPLE.

WAYS WE CULTIVATE OUR DIVINE FEMININE ENERGY ARE BY COOKING, HOMEMAKING, TAKING CARE OF CHILDREN, GARDENING, PAINTING, SINGING, DANCING, LAUGHING, MEDITATING, AND EVEN GIVING BIRTH. THE ARTICLE THEN RECOMMENDS

READING "THE ARTIST'S WAY' BY JULIA CAMERON. SHE CONTINUES BY SAY THAT IT DIVES INTO THE SPIRITUALITY BEHIND CREATIVITY. THIS CAN BE ILLUMINATING & HEALING FOR SOMEONE TRYING TO REGAIN AWARENESS OF THEIR DIVINE FEMININE ENERGY.

2. *WARRIOR SPIRIT* = THE SECOND OF THE 7 CHARACTERISTICS OF FEMININE ENERGY IS THE WARRIOR SPIRIT. CONTRARY TO WHAT SEEMS, THE DIVINE FEMININE IS PRETTY BAD ASS. FEMALE BLACK WIDOWS ARE WELL-KNOWN FOR FEEDING ON THEIR PARTNERS IMMEDIATELY AFTER SEX.

MANY OTHER SPECIES EAT THEIR CHILDREN IN DIRE CIRCUMSTANCES.

THE FEMININE IS THE GIVER AND SOMETIMES THE TAKER OF LIFE. DIVINE FEMININE ENERGY TENDS TO EMASCULATE AND DEVOUR THE MASCULINE ENERGY WHEN WE DO NOT KNOW HOW TO WORK WITH IT. WE TEND TO IMPRISON THE MASCULINE WITH JEALOUSY AND DOMINATE AND EMASCULATE THE PROTECTIVE NATURE.

IN THE TAROT, IT IS REPRESENTED BY THE DEATH CARD. THE CARD REPRESENTS PROFOUND CHANGE, NOT BEING COMPLACENT, STEPPING UP TO THE PLATE, AND TAKING WHAT IS OURS. WORKING TOWARD ALIGNMENT WITH OUR TRUEST SELVES AND NATURE, THE DIVINE FEMININE ENERGY IS THE GREATEST CREATIVE FORCE OF ALL. IF GOD WERE A

PERSON, IT WOULD SURELY BE FEMININE.

THIS WARRIOR SPIRIT IS A SUBTLE, STEADY CURRENT THAT BECOMES ILLUMINATED WHEN WE DON'T LISTEN TO OUR INTUITION. THE DIVINE FEMININE ENERGY IS PRONE TO CONSTANT STRUGGLES & OVERCOMING, AS IT SEEKS PERPETUAL EVOLUTION. IT GUIDES US TO ELIMINATE WHAT DOES NOT WORK AND INCREASE WHAT DOES. WE TEND TO ATTRACT BOTH PLEASANT AND UNPLEASANT OPPORTUNITIES FOR TRANSFORMATION INTO OUR LIVES THROUGH THIS ENERGY. WHETHER IT BE IN THE FORM OF CHANGE WITHIN OUR FAMILIES, RELATIONSHIPS, CAREERS, MOTHERHOOD, OR EVEN HEALTH.

WHEN THINGS FALL APART, THERE IS USUALLY A MUCH HIGHER PURPOSE.

TO WORK WITH THIS ENERGY, WE MUST ACCEPT THIS FACT AND LEARN TO IDENTIFY THE LESSON IN IT WITHOUT REACTING EMOTIONALLY. WE HAVE ATTRACTED EVERYTHING IN OUR EXPERIENCE, AND INSTEAD OF RESISTING, WE MUST FIND GRATITUDE IN THE SITUATION.

IN ALCHEMY WHEN WE WANT TO TURN LEAD INTO GOLD, WE FIRST HAVE TO ALLOW A HOT FIRE TO BLACKEN AND BURN THE LEAD. THIS SEPARATES THE PURE MATTER FROM THE IMPURE MATTER. THE ONLY THING LEFT IS THE STRONGEST MATERIAL.

ALCHEMY OF THE DIVINE FEMININE WORKS THE SAME WAY.

WE MUST ALLOW OURSELVES TO GROW THROUGH WHAT WE MANIFEST, AS WE ARE LEARNING AND EXPANDING BECAUSE OF IT. AS A RESULT, WE BECOME BETTER, STRONGER, AND MORE SENTIENT.

KALI MA CALLED THE "DARK MOTHER" IS THE HINDU GODDESS OF CREATION, PRESERVATION, AND DESTRUCTION. SHE PERSONIFIES THE DIVINE FEMININE. SHE REPRESENTS A DEIFIED ASPECT WITHIN US ALL, RATHER THAN A DEITY THAT IS WORSHIPPED OUTSIDE OF OURSELVES/ SHE IS OFTEN DEPICTED OVER HER DEAD CONSORT, SHIVA

DEVOURING HIS ENTRAILS WHILE HER YONI SEXUALLY DEVOURS HIS PENIS. THIS IS ANALOGOUS TO THE TENDENCY OF THE DIVINE FEMININE ENERGY IN BLACK WIDOWS AND OTHER SPECIES....

IN INDIA, THE DIVINE FEMININE IS CONNECTED WITH BOTH LIFE AND BIRTH, AND INTEGRALLY CONNECTED WITH DEATH AND DESTRUCTION. THE IMPORTANCE OF THE DEPICTION OF KALI MA AS THE LIFE-GIVER, PRESERVER, AND DESTROYER HAVE BEEN DISMISSED OVER THE CENTURIES. MEN TYPICALLY FEAR THIS KIND OF POWER WITHIN WOMEN AND HAVE USED PHYSICAL STRENGTH AND DOMINANCE TO CREATE MORE PATERNALISTIC CULTURES.

The article by DF Alchemy 2019 continues describing the warrior spirit of the Divine Feminine by stating that Interpretations of Kali Ma focus on the most destructive aspects of the Goddess and portray her as fearsome and evil. As we know, there is always a dual nature to everything per the Law of Duality.

3. *DEEP SENSE OF JUSTICE, BALANCE, & MORALITY.*

The article continues by mentioning The book "The Four Agreements" which talks about how we have chosen to believe what we have been programmed to believe. It is so difficult to recognize & change

OUR CORE BELIEFS AS WE LIVE THROUGH THEM IN EVERY ENCOUNTER, EVERY DA. AN OPEN MIND IS SO IMPORTANT FOR SPIRITUAL GROWTH BECAUSE IT ALLOWS US TO EXPERIMENT WITH NEW IDEAS, INSTEAD OF FEELING SELF-RIGHTEOUS AND JUDGMENTAL AND MANIFESTING A REALITY THE SAME AS THE PEOPLE WHO GAVE US THESE BELIEFS.

THE DIVINE FEMININE HAS A STRONG SENSE OF JUSTICE, BALANCE, AND MORALITY. ITS ALWAYS TRYING TO LOOK PAST WHAT SEEMS TO THE TRUTH OF THE MATTER. IN THE MODERN WORLD WE HAVE BEEN PROGRAMMED TO REACT AND RESPOND THROUGH OBJECTIVITY RATHER THAN ENGAGE

WITH OTHERS WHO MAY NOT SEE THINGS THE SAME AS WE DO.

AS THE DIVINE FEMININE, YOU'LL FIND YOURSELF ENGAGING OR EVEN INITIATING DEEP CONVERSATIONS. WITHOUT ALCHEMY OF THE DIVINE FEMININE ENERGY, WE THEN DEBATING THE MERITS OF IDEAS AND CHARACTER ASSASSINATION, WE UNLEASH OUR WARRIOR SPIRIT. IT IS OUR TENDENCY TO SEEK TRUTH BUT WITHOUT A GREAT AMOUNT OF AWARENESS WE UNLEASH OUR WARRIOR SPIRIT.

THIS PUT THIS TO THE TEST CALL UP ANY ONE OF YOUR NOT-SO-LIKE-MINDED GIRLFRIENDS OR FEMALE RELATIVES AND SEE IF THEY CAN CARRY

ON A CONVERSATION FOR 10 MINUTES WITHOUT BECOMING EMOTIONALLY REACTIVE.

4. *PASSIVE RESISTANCE* = ALCHEMY THEN CONTINUES THE ARTICLE BY SAYING AND I QUOTE "I DON'T KNOW MANY WOMEN WHO PREFER A HEATED DEBATE OVER PEACE AND TRANQUILITY. WE ALL HAVE BOTH MASCULINE AND FEMININE ENERGY, BUT I PREFER PASSIVITY OVER DOMINANCE." SHE CONTINUES WITH I DON'T MEAN SUBMISSIVENESS; I MEAN AVOIDING CONFRONTATION, AND DISSOLVING CONFLICTS BEFORE THEY ESCALATE. PASSIVITY IS DEFINED AS "ACCEPTING OR ALLOWING WHAT HAPPENS OR WHAT OTHERS DO WITHOUT ACTIVE RESPONSE OR RESISTANCE."

THIS IS GENERALLY A WEAKNESS IN

PATERNALISTIC CULTURE. HOWEVER, THE ANCIENT EGYPTIANS, TEACH THAT "IT IS PASSIVE RESISTANCE FROM THE HELM TIS THE DIVINE FEMININE AT WORK. HAT STEERS THE BOAT. WOMAN ARE KNOWN TO BE MANIPULATIVE WHICH INVOLVES PASSIVE RESISTANCE. TO BE ABLE TO GET YOUR WAY WITHOUT FIGHTING ABOUT IT IS THE DIVINE FEMININE AT WORK. THE DIVINE FEMININE WORKS AT THE SUB-CONSCIOUS LEVEL AND DOES NOT HAVE TO BECOME VIOLENT OR AGGRESSIVE TO MANIFEST ITS DESIRES.

5. *STRONGER AWARENESS OF THOUGHTS AND FEELINGS* = EVERYONE SHOULD KNOW THE SOURCE OF THEIR OWN THOUGHTS AND FEELINGS. A MAJOR ONE OF THE 7

CHARACTERISTICS OF FEMININE ENERGY IS BEING AWARE OF OUR EMOTIONS, AND SUDDEN SHIFTS IN EMOTIONS. UNFORTUNATELY, MEN ARE DISCOURAGED FROM EXPRESSING THEIR EMOTIONS FROM THE TIME THEY'RE BORN. WE ALL CONTAIN BOTH DIVINE FEMININE AND DIVINE MASCULINE ENERGIES, WITHOUT THE YIN, THERE WOULD BE NO YANG.

THE ARTICLE CONTINUES DESCRIBING THE DIVINE FEMININE, BY STATING THAT LUCKILY, WE WOMEN TEND TO BE MORE SENSITIVE AND AWARE OF EMOTIONAL CHANGES. NOT ONLY ARE WE ENCOURAGED IN OUR SENSITIVITIES, BUT WE ALSO EXPERIENCE HORMONAL CHANGES ALL THROUGHOUT OUR LIVES: IN PUBERTY, ADOLESCENCE, PMS, CHILDBEARING, AND MENOPAUSE. EMOTIONS

ARE COMPLETELY REACTIVE IN NATURE, INVOLVING A SUBJECTIVE EXPERIENCE, A PHYSIOLOGICAL RESPONSE AND A BEHAVIORAL, EXPRESSIVE RESPONSE.

THEY DO NOT EXIST IN THE UNSEEN, UNMANIFEST, BUT THE UNDERLYING CAUSE OF THE EMOTIONS CAN BE ADDRESSED IN THE SUB-CONSCIOUS. WOMEN TEND TO BE MUCH MORE ADVANCED EMOTIONALLY. WE TAKE PRIDE IN BEING VULNERABLE AND ARE MUCH MORE INTIMATE WITH ONE ANOTHER. THERE IS NO DEFINITIVE LINE BETWEEN A STRICTLY HETEROSEXUAL WOMAN AND A SEXUALLY FLUID WOMAN. MEN ON THE OTHER HAND ARE MUCH MORE POLAR. THEY ARE DISCOURAGED FROM EXPERIENCING AND UNDERSTANDING THEIR

FEELINGS AND THEREFORE ARE DISCONNECTED FROM THE SOURCE. ""HOLDING ONTO ANGER IS LIKE DRINKING POISON AND EXPECTING THE OTHER PERSON TO DIE." ~BUDDHA.

EMOTIONS ARE COMPLETELY REACTIVE IN NATURE, INVOLVING A SUBJECTIVE EXPERIENCE, A PHYSIOLOGICAL RESPONSE, AND A BEHAVIORAL, EXPRESSIVE RESPONSE. THEY DO NOT EXIST IN THE UNSEEN, UNMANIFEST, BUT THE UNDERLYING CAUSE OF THE EMOTIONS CAN BE ADDRESSED IN THE SUB-CONSCIOUS. WOMEN TEND TO BE MUCH MORE ADVANCED EMOTIONALLY. WE TAKE PRIDE IN BEING VULNERABLE AND ARE MUCH MORE INTIMATE WITH ONE ANOTHER. THERE IS NO DEFINITIVE

LINE BETWEEN A STRICTLY HETEROSEXUAL WOMAN AND A SEXUALLY FLUID WOMAN.

MEN ON THE OTHER HAND ARE MUCH MORE POLAR. THEY ARE DISCOURAGED FROM EXPERIENCING AND UNDERSTANDING THEIR FEELINGS AND THEREFORE ARE DISCONNECTED FROM THE SOURCE. "HOLDING ONTO ANGER IS LIKE DRINKING POISON AND EXPECTING THE OTHER PERSON TO DIE" (BUDDHA.")

6. *HAVING A MINI-SIDED PERSONALITY*

AS WOMEN, WE PLAY MANY ROLES. WIFE, MOTHER, DAUGHTER, SISTER, GIRLFRIEND...NOT TO MENTION THE LESS APPRECIATED ROLES LIKE BABY MAMA, SIDE CHICK,

MENTOR, WORKPLACE HOTTIE, SECRETARY, SISTER-IN-LAW, NANNY, MAID, COOK, DANCER, ENTREPRENEUR, OR ELDER. AS THE CREATIVE ENERGY, WE SHAPE-SHIFT TO FIT THE NEEDS OF EACH CIRCUMSTANCE. ONE OF THE IMPORTANT CHARACTERISTICS, OF FEMININE ENERGY IS THE ABILITY TO PLAY MANY ROLES. ALONG WITH THE MANY ROLES WE PLAY, WE ALSO TAKE ON THE PERSONALITY TRAITS. REQUIRED TO BE SUCCESSFUL.

ALCHEMY, THEN CONTINUES THE ARTICLE STATING THAT "MY MOTHER COULD BE ON THE PHONE WITH HER BOSS USING HER CORPORATE PERSONALITY AND THEN SNAP AT MY BROTHER AND I IN THE BACKSEAT, TELLING

US TO STOP ARGUING." AS A MOTHER MYSELF, I TOO HAVE A CORPORATE PERSONALITY AND VOICE THAT I USE FOR BUSINESS AFFAIRS, HOWEVER, THAT VOICE CAN CHANGE INSTANTLY WHEN DEALING WITH THE BEHAVIORS OF UNRULY CHILDREN.

ALCHEMY THEN STATES "HISTORICALLY, WOMEN HAVE ALWAYS HAD TO PLAY MANY ROLES. IN THE 18TH DYNASTY IN IN EGYPT, THE PHARAOH HATSHEPSUT LED MILITARY CAMPAIGNS, REBUILT MONUMENTS, AND CULTIVATED BOTH HER HUSBAND AND STEP-SONS AS KINGS."

MODERN WOMEN SEEM TO HAVE EVEN MORE ROLES TO PLAY, AS THE SINGLE MOM' ARCHETYPE DID NOT EXIST IN ANTIQUITY. SO,

MANY OF US HAVE TO PLAY THE MOTHER AND FATHER TO OUR CHILDREN. WE HUNT, PROVIDE, PROTECT, GIVE BIRTH, CULTIVATE, NURTURE, AND SHE'LL MAKE BANANA PUDDING. GIVE A WOMAN A HOUSE, AND SHE'LL MAKE IT A HOME. GIVE A WOMAN SPERM, AND SHE'LL MAKE A HUMAN BEING. ONLY A WOMAN CAN TAKE WHATEVER LIFE GIVES HER AND MAKE IT BETTER.

7. *FEELING THE NEED TO SELF-SACRIFICE TO REMAIN VIRTUOUS.*

FIRST, LET ME CLARIFY... THERE IS NO SUCH THING AS SACRIFICE. EVERYTHING IS AN ENERGETIC EXCHANGE. WHEN IT SEEMS YOU ARE CARRYING THE LOAD FOR SOMEONE ELSE, YOU ARE

REALLY PROJECTING A REALITY YOU'VE LIKELY BEEN LIVING IN YOU FOR A LONG TIME. AS AN ALCHEMIST OF THE DIVINE FEMININE ENERGY, IT IS YOUR JOB TO ABSORB UNCONSCIOUSNESS AND TRANSFORM IT. BY CHOOSING TO "SACRIFICE" WE'RE ENERGETICALLY SAYING EITHER "I CAN HANDLE MORE AS I AM STRONGER AND MORE EQUIPPED." OR "I AM TOO WEAK TO SAY NO BECAUSE IT SEEMS THAT CIRCUMSTANCES ARE OUT OF MY CONTROL." EITHER WAY, THIS IS A SELF-=CENTERED REALITY YOU'RE EXPERIENCING. I'VE KNOWN PEOPLE TO SACRIFICE MONEY SO THEIR KID CAN ATTEND PRIVATE SCHOOL; IT WAS NOT THE CHILD'S CHOICE BUT THEIR

OWN, AND USUALLY FOR PRESTIGE PURPOSES.

SHE CONTINUES BY SAYING, "I'VE KNOWN PARENTS TO GO INTO DEBT BUYING CHRISTMAS PRESENTS; IT WAS NOT BECAUSE THE KID FORCED THEM TO GET A WALMART CARD, BUT THEY FELT PRESSURED TO LIVE A CERTAIN LIFESTYLE AND PARTICIPATE IN A HIGHLY COMMERCIALIZED HOLIDAY. I'VE KNOWN PEOPLE TO THE LAST OF THEIR SAVINGS WHEN THEY CAN'T PAY THEIR BILLS BECAUSE THEY DIDN'T WANT TO EMBARRASS THEMSELVES IN FRONT OF THE CONGREGATION. THIS TENDENCY FOR SELF-SACRIFICE IS A CHARACTERISTIC OF FEMININE ENERGY FOR SURE. IN THE WILD WE WOULD SACRIFICE FOR OUR

CHILDREN SO THEY MIGHT SURVIVE ANOTHER DAY; SACRIFICE IS NATURAL.

WE JUST DON'T WANT TO GET TRAPPED ON THE ILLUSORY SIDE OF IT, THINKING WE WILL ATTRACT GREAT THINGS THROUGH SACRIFICE. IT ISN'T ABOUT THAT, AS SACRIFICE INVOLVES MORE RECEIVING THAN GIVING ENERGETICALLY. WE MAY GIVE OUR TIME OR MONEY AND RECEIVE THANKS. BUT ON AN ENERGETIC LEVEL, WE GIVE GRATITUDE AND RECEIVE WORSHIP/ DEVOTION. THROUGH THE OTHER PERSON'S GRATITUDE. WITHOUT PROPER CULTIVATION, AND UNDERSTANDING OF UNIVERSAL LAW, WE END UP TAKING MORE THAN WE'RE GIVING OFF BY FEELING ENTITLED TO

PRAISE THROUGH OUR "SACRIFICE."

ALCHEMY FINISHES THE ARTICLE BY SAYING "I'VE KNOWN PEOPLE TO TITHE THE LAST OF THEIR SAVINGS WHEN THEY CAN'T PAY THEIR BILLS BECAUSE THEY DIDN'T WANT TO EMBARRASS THEMSELVES IN FRONT OF THE CONGREGATION. THIS TENDENCY FOR SELF-=SACRIFICE, IS A CHARACTERISTIC OF FEMININE ENERGY FOR SURE. IN THE WILD WE WOULD SACRIFICE FOR OUR CHILDREN SO THEY MIGHT SURVIVE ANOTHER DAY. SACRIFICE IS NATURAL....

IN MY OPINION, THE TRAITS OF THE DIVINE MASCULINE AND FEMININE WERE DESCRIBED IN THE ALCHEMY 2019

ARTICLE. THE ARTICLE BEST CAPTURED THE CHARACTERISTICS OF BOTH TWINS IN ESSENCE.

CHAPTER 19

AWARENESS

In the weeks and months that followed the twins last physical encounter where both lovers became awakened to their Kundalini Energy, barely any communication took place between them. Rhea picked up the telephone with intents to call Rico on several occasions as did he, but both only ended up hanging up before the ringing began. After so many weeks Rhea decided to throw herself into work, home life and personal projects. However, living in such a small community where most families knew each other, when

THE RUMOR MILL WOULD BEGIN TO TURN, IT USUALLY REACHED THE VAST MAJORITIES OF MAHOGANY VALLEY OCCUPANTS.

RHEA SOON BEGIN HEARING DIFFERENT RUMORS FROM THE GOSSIPING RUMOR-MILL ABOUT RICO'S LESS THAN STELLAR DEALINGS WITH ALL TYPES OF NEGATIVE ENERGIES. AT FIRST, SHE'D HAD A DISBELIEVING ATTITUDE ABOUT THE STRAIGHT RAUNCHY BEHAVIOR SHE'D BEEN INFORMED ABOUT. BUT AFTER PEOPLE SHE KNEW AND RESPECTED CAME FORWARD WITH ACCUSATIONS ABOUT DRUGS, ALCOHOLISM, STRIPPERS AND LADIES OF THE NIGHT, SHE BEGAN TO WONDER JUST WHO IN THE HELL THIS MAN SHE HAD COME TO LOVE AND RESPECT TRULY WAS BEHIND THE MASKS AND FALSE WORDS.

RHEA DECIDED TO SILENTLY INVESTIGATE MATTERS FOR HERSELF TO FIND CLARITY AND PEACE OF MIND. SHE SOON DISCOVERED THAT ALL RUMORS WERE NOT ACCURATE, BUT

SOME WERE INDEED THE CASE AND POINT. SHE ALSO FOUND OUT THAT HE HAD BEEN PARTICIPATING IN SEXUAL DEVIANT BEHAVIOR WITH MORE THAN 2 PARTY SITUATIONS AND WAS ALSO INVOLVED IN OTHER RELATIONSHIPS BEYOND THEIRS. SHE DIDN'T QUITE KNOW WHEN ALL THE DARK BEHAVIOR BEGAN OR IF SOMETHING THAT HAPPENED BETWEEN THEM HAD TRIGGERED IT, BUT WHAT SHE DID KNOW WAS HER TWIN WAS IN TROUBLE PHYSICALLY, MENTALLY AND ALSO PSYCHOLOGICALLY AND HE NEEDED HELP!

RHEA DIDN'T KNOW IT AT THE TIME, BUT SHE SOON FOUND ANSWERS AS TO WHY RICO HAD SHUT OFF THEIR CONNECTION AND BEGAN VIBRATING IN HIS LOWER SELF-IMAGE AS OPPOSED TO ASCENDING TO REACH HIS HIGHEST LEVEL OF VIBRATION TO CLAIM THE STATUS OF THE DIVINE MASCULINE ON THE PATH THAT GOD HAD PRE-DESTINED HIM TO FOLLOW WITH HER. SHE CONTINUED DOING RESEARCH ON THE DIVINE MASCULINE

ENERGY AND THIS TIME WHAT SHE FOUND PROPELLED HER IMMEDIATELY INTO WARRIOR SPIRIT THE 2ND OF THE DIVINE FEMININE CHARACTERISTICS.

RHEA NEEDED TO MAKE A PLAN SO SHE DECIDED TO DO AS SHE HAD ALWAYS DONE AND SEEK OUT DIVINE DIRECTION AND PROTECTION FROM GOD AND WAIT ON CLEAR INSTRUCTIONS FROM HIM. RHEA LEANED ON HER EDUCATION AND KNOWLEDGE OF THE HUMAN PSYCHE. ONCE SHE UNDERSTOOD WHAT WAS MOTIVATING THIS SUDDEN DARK NIGHT ENERGY, SHE WAS BETTER ABLE TO PRAY FOR THE THINGS THAT WOULD ALLOW HER TO STAY CONNECTED BY TELEPATHY AND INTUITION.

RHEA HAD ALWAYS BEEN AWARE OF HER INTUITIVE GIFTS EVEN AS A CHILD WHEN SHE PREDICTED CERTAIN THINGS TO HER FAMILY BEFORE THEY HAPPENED. BUT BECAUSE SHE FOUND THEM TO BE A LITTLE FRIGHTENING TO HERSELF AND HER FAMILY, SHE LEARNED TO IGNORE THEM AND KEEP

THEM HIDDEN WHERE NO ONE COULD TELL SHE HAD THEM.

RHEA FOUND THAT THOSE SAME INTUITIVE GIFTS SHE HAD FOUGHT TO KEEP HIDDEN FOR SO LONG HAD SOMEHOW COME BACK IN FULL FORCE ONCE SHE STARTED DEALING WITH HER TWIN FLAME. IT OCCURRED TO HER ALSO THAT IF THEY WERE TRULY TWINS, HE WOULD PROBABLY POSSESS SOME IF NOT ALL OF THE SAME GIFTS SHE HAD. BUT, IF HE HADN'T YET BEEN "AWAKENED" TO HIS HIGHER SELF THEN MAYBE HIS GIFTS WERE NOT RECOGNIZED. OR, IF HE WERE USING THEM FOR DARK MAGIC OR THE OCCULT OR ANYTHING THAT OPERATES IN DARK SPIRITUAL ENERGIES NOT ONLY WOULD HE HAVE TO DEAL WITH KARMA FOR IT, BUT GOD MIGHT ALSO DEEM IT NECESSARY TO STRIP HIM OF ALL POWER UNTIL HE AWAKENED, ASCENDED, AND BEGAN WALKING IN HIS RIGHT PATH.

RHEA SPENT SEVERAL DAYS PRAYING, TALKING TO GOD, STUDYING,

LEARNING, HEALING, GROWING AND ASCENDING AS SHE HAD BECOME AWAKENED TO HER HIGHER SELF AND NOW UNDERSTOOD HER TRUE PURPOSE IN LIFE. SHE NOW REALIZED WHAT THE TWIN FLAMES TRUE PATH WAS, AND WHY OUR ALMIGHTY FATHER HAD GIFTED HER AND PROBABLY HER TWIN AS WELL WITH THE SPECIAL GIFTS SHE DISCOVERED MORE ABOUT EACH DAY.

AS SHE ASCENDED TOWARDS HER HIGHEST SELF SPIRITUALLY, SHE NOW UNDERSTOOD HER POWER AND KNEW INSTINCTIVELY THAT TOGETHER, AND IN THEIR FULL POWER, THE TWINS WOULD BE UNSTOPPABLE IN EVERY AREA OF THEIR LIVES. GOD HAD SHOWN HER WHAT THEY WERE MEANT TO DO, AND HE WOULD HAVE GIVEN THEM FULL ABUNDANCE IN HEALTH, WEALTH, CREATIVITY, UNCONDITIONAL LOVE, HEALING HIS PEOPLE THROUGH MUSIC AND OTHER GIFTS THEY POSSESSED.

Now that she understood the path they were meant to be on together, she knew she had to do something to try and get Rico back on track to his awakening before it was too late.

CHAPTER 20

DIVINE MASCULINE AND THE KARMICS

DURING THE SPRING MONTHS, RICO WOULD NOT ALLOW HIMSELF TO REACH OUT TO RHEA NO MATTER HOW MUCH HE MISSED HER. HE THREW HIMSELF INTO HIS OLD LOW VIBRATING WAYS. HE HUNG OUT WITH A CERTAIN CROWD WHO LIVED LIFE WITHOUT VALUES MORALS OR DISCIPLINE. THEY FREQUENTED STRIP CLUBS PICKING OUT WOMEN WHO DIDN'T MIND DOING WHATEVER THEY WANTED FOR A PRICE. HE BEGAN FEEDING HABITS THAT COST HIM MOST OF HIS SAVINGS BUT NEVERTHELESS HE CONTINUED TO PARTICIPATE IN

3RD PARTY SITUATIONS AND SEVERAL PARTY ORGIES.

RICO ALLOWED HIMSELF TO REMAIN LOST IN HIS LUSTS AND LOW VIBRATIONAL ENERGY FIGHTING HIS FEELINGS DAILY SO THAT HE WOULDN'T HAVE TO FACE HIS EMOTIONAL DEMONS. DAYS TURNED INTO WEEKS AND WEEKS TO MONTHS. RICO MOVED IN WITH ONE OF THE KARMIC WOMEN HE HAD KNOWN SINCE HIGH SCHOOL. HE THOUGHT THIS WOMAN WAS HIS SOUL MATE AND THAT WHAT HE FELT FOR RHEA WAS ONLY LUST. BUT NO MATTER HOW HE TRIED TO FORGET THE CONNECTION, HE COULD NOT GET HER NOR THE TIME THEY SPENT TOGETHER OUT OF HIS MIND. HE FOUND HIMSELF LYING AWAKE AT NIGHT WONDERING WHAT SHE WAS DOING OR JUST WHOM SHE WAS SEEING NOW.

RICO WAS SURPRISED TO FIND THAT HE COULDN'T STOP HIMSELF FROM BECOMING ANGRY AND JEALOUS THINKING ABOUT WHO MIGHT HAVE

ACCESS TO RHEA. HE FOUND HIMSELF THINKING ABOUT HER WHEN A CERTAIN SONG WAS PLAYING OR WHEN HE SAW SOMEONE WITH A HAIRSTYLE OR CLOTHING THAT REMINDED HIM OF HER. FINALLY, RICO WENT TO HIS BEAUTIFUL SISTER TO HAVE A HEART-TO-HEART CONVERSATION AND TO GET A FEMALE PROSPECTIVE ON THIS SITUATION.

HE SPOKE TO HER CANDIDLY AND LAID HIS WHOLE HAND OUT TO HER. HIS SISTER LISTENED TO HIM WITHOUT INTERRUPTION BEFORE COMMENTING. SHE TOLD HER BROTHER THAT HE FIRST NEEDED TO SLOW DOWN AND GET HIS SHIT TOGETHER. "YOU ARE NOT GETTING ANY YOUNGER RICO AND YOU ARE ENTIRELY TOO OLD TO BE OUT HERE DOING WHAT YOU HAVE BEEN DOING, YOU NEED TO STOP BEFORE YOU CATCH SOMETHING THERE IS NO CURE FOR."

RICO LISTENED INTENTLY TO HIS SISTER AND SPOKE HIS TRUTH TO HER ABOUT THE MAGICAL CONNECTION HE

SHARED WITH RHEA. HIS SISTER TOLD HIM THAT THAT RELATIONSHIP NEEDED TO BE RE-VISITED HE SHOULD HAVE NEVER DISREGARDED A RELATIONSHIP THAT HAD THAT SO MUCH POTENTIAL. RICO'S SISTER MIA HAD GIVEN HIM MANY THINGS TO THINK ABOUT AND ALL THAT SHE SAID WAS CERTAINLY WEIGHING HEAVILY ON HIS MIND AS HE LEFT THAT DAY.

WHEN HE THOUGHT ABOUT RHEA AND HOW THE ENERGY BETWEEN THEM WAS STILL SO STRONG AFTER ALL THIS TIME, HE KNEW HE HAD NO OTHER CHOICE BUT TO SUCK IT UP AND REACH OUT TO HER ONCE MORE. RICO THOUGHT ABOUT HOW TO BEST HANDLE THE SITUATION WITH RHEA. HE STAYED LOCKED IN HIS HEAD BOTH DAY AND NIGHT REHEARSING DIFFERENT WAYS TO APOLOGIZE TO HER AND ASK IF THEY COULD REKINDLE THE RELATIONSHIP.

HE REALIZED WHAT HE WAS CONTEMPLATING WAS REALLY A LONGSHOT BECAUSE HE DIDN'T KNOW

IF SHE WAS SEEING ANYONE NOW, OR IN A SERIOUS OR COMMITTED RELATIONSHIP AS HE CURRENTLY WAS. RICO BEGAN TO TRY AND TAME HIMSELF DOWN A LITTLE AS HIS SISTER MIA'S WORDS BEGAN TO RESONATE IN HIS THOUGHTS AT NIGHT WHILE TRYING HIS BEST TO SLEEP. HE KNEW SHE WAS RIGHT AND THAT HIS BEHAVIOR AT HIS AGE WAS A RECIPE FOR DISASTER.

RICO THOUGHT ABOUT THE BEAUTIFUL WOMAN ACROSS TOWN WHO ONLY TRIED TO LOVE HIM AND BE THERE FOR HIM, THE ONE HE'D RUN AWAY FROM BECAUSE HIS FEELINGS FOR HER BECAME TOO INTENSE AND MORE THAN HE COULD HANDLE AT THE TIME. WHAT IF SHE NEVER WANTED TO LAY EYES ON THE LIKES OF HIS SORRY, IMMATURE ACTING ASS AGAIN? HE COULDN'T BARE THE THOUGHT OF THAT. THAT WOULDN'T BE SOMETHING HE COULD EVER ALLOW TO HAPPEN. HE'D FIGHT LIKE HELL TO WIN HER LOVE BACK IF NECESSARY.

THAT NIGHT INSTEAD OF HANGING OUT WITH HIS TRIBE, HE LISTENED TO HIS FAVORITE MUSIC AND ALLOWED HIMSELF TO REMINISCE OVER THE TIMES HE SHARED WITH THE WOMAN HE WAS GROWING TO LOVE. HE THOUGHT HE WOULD NEVER EXPERIENCE THIS TYPE OF FEELINGS AGAIN BECAUSE IN THE PASS HE'D BEEN PRETTY UNLUCKY IN LOVE. WHAT HE FELT FOR THE KARMIC WOMAN WHOM HE SHARED A HOME WITH DIDN'T EVEN COME CLOSE TO HIS FEELINGS FOR RHEA.

SOMEHOW, AND WITH COMPLETE UNAWARENESS, HE DIDN'T SEE HOW HIS BEHAVIOR WAS CHANGING UNTIL ONE DAY HE WAS CONFRONTED BY HIS KARMIC PARTNER ASKING WHAT WAS WRONG WITH HIM? RICO IMMEDIATELY BECAME DEFENSIVE WITH HER ASKING WHAT SHE MEANT AND ACCUSING HER OF BEING DRAMATIC.

TO HIM ANY WOMAN WHO CHALLENGED HIS POSITION OR DISAGREED WITH HIM WAS AUTOMATICALLY LABELED A

DRAMA QUEEN. SHE ARGUED WITH HIM FOR A WHILE ASKING WHY HE HADN'T BEEN HANGING OUT WITH HER AND THE OTHER MEN AND WOMEN IN THEIR GROUP? RICO SIMPLY WAIVED HER QUESTIONS OFF AND IGNORED HER.

LATE SPRING TURNED INTO EARLY SUMMER AND RICO COULD NO LONGER DENY THE ACHING, LONGING, PASSIONATE FEELINGS HE HAD DAILY FOR RHEA. ALTHOUGH HE'D STARTED BACK HANGING OUT WITH THE GUYS AND TAKING HIS SEXUAL PLEASURES OUT ON THE STRIPPERS, CLUB KARMICS AND ONE-NIGHT STANDS, HE COULDN'T FIND ANYONE WITH THE SAME PASSIONATE CONNECTION HE'D EXPERIENCED WITH RHEA.

ONE NIGHT AFTER COMING DOWN FROM A WILD WEEKEND OF DRINKING, SMOKING, DRUGGING AND PARTYING HE GOT DOWN ON HIS KNEES AND ASKED GOD TO HELP HIM FIGHT HIS WAY BACK TO THE WOMAN HE LOVED, AND IF THIS WAS THE PATH HE WAS MEANT TO BE ON, HE ASKED

THE ALMIGHTY TO SEND HIM A SIGN. THE NEXT DAY, RHEA CALLED TO ASK HOW HE WAS DOING AND TO SAY HOW MUCH SHE MISSED HIM. HE KNEW WITHOUT A DOUBT AFTER THAT, THAT THIS RELATIONSHIP WAS INDEED DIVINELY GUIDED, AND HE WOULD TRY HARD NOT TO MESS IT UP AGAIN.

CHAPTER 21

KARMIC INTERFERENCES

Rico finally worked up the nerve to continue calling his beloved lady love and found that she was equally anxious to resume the relationship with him. In the weeks that followed they tried to make up for lost time. They went on dates both large and small. The twins were so happy to be together they even made a loving, cuddling production of a visit to the Dairy Queen for ice cream. They appreciated the time they spent together seeming to never want to remember the pain of being separate ever again.

DURING THEIR RECONCILIATION, RICO DID ALL HE COULD TO TRY AND MAKE UP FOR THE HEARTBREAK HE CAUSED RHEA BY DISAPPEARING ON HER. THAT ALL CHANGED AFTER A HUSHED CONVERSATION HE TOOK ON HIS MOBILE PHONE LATE ONE EVENING. RHEA WAS A LITTLE SUSPICIOUS ABOUT THE CALL BUT HAVING TRUST IN HER MAN SHE KEPT QUIET ABOUT HER CONCERNS. AS IT TURNED OUT, SHE WAS VERY RIGHT TO BE CONCERNED AND THE RECONCILIATION THAT HAD BROUGHT THE DIVINE COUPLE SO MUCH JOY, TURNED OUT TO BE VERY SHORT-LIVED.

WEEKS WENT BY AND RHEA ONLY SAW RICO A FEW TIMES IN A LONG SPAN OF TIME. WHEN HE DROPPED BY, HE WOULD ONLY STAY BRIEFLY AND WHEN SHE CONFRONTED HIM ABOUT HIS BEHAVIOR, HE EITHER EVADED THE QUESTIONS OR BECAME VERY QUIET NEVER ANSWERING ANYTHING SHE ASKED OR NEVER DEFINING EXACTLY WHAT THIS RELATIONSHIP HAD BECOME. AS A RESULT, SHE

BEGAN TO LOSE ALL FAITH AND HOPE IN THE CONNECTION AND SIMPLY THREW HERSELF INTO HER WORK AND WITH FRIENDS AS A SUPPORT SYSTEM AGAIN.

AS SPRING TURNED INTO SUMMER, RHEA BEGAN TO EXPLORE MORE VENUES IN TOWN. SHE STARTED TO HEAR RUMORS AGAIN THAT WERE LESS THAN FLATTERING PERTAINING TO RICO. USUALLY, SHE DIDN'T PAY MUCH ATTENTION TO NASTY RUMORS OR GOSSIPING BUT THESE WERE WORTH INVESTIGATING SO SHE WOULD ONCE AGAIN HAVE A CLEAR PICTURE OF WHAT HAPPENED SO ABRUPTLY BETWEEN HER AND RICO AND WHY THIS BEHAVIOR KEPT REARING ITS UGLY HEAD IN A CONNECTION THAT SEEMED SO OBVIOUSLY SPECIAL TO BOTH PEOPLE.

RICO BEGAN TO PICK UP WHERE HE LEFT OFF LAST YEAR WHEN HIS RELATIONSHIP WENT SOUTH DUE TO HIS ACTIONS WITH KARMIC RELATIONSHIPS AND TOXIC FRIENDS.

Rico continued down this same destructive path for weeks never considering the hurt and deceit he brought to this relationship with Rhea.

Eventually, Rhea became tired of the neglect and the disrespect. Being an honest God-fearing woman, she gave him time to come forward and tell her what was happening to their connection but still he refused to talk about anything that pertained to the double life he was living.

Finally, Rhea went to the one source she had always depended on for guidance and direction when things in her life became difficult or challenging. Her source was her Heavenly Father. She'd always maintained a close relationship with the Almighty since she was a young woman and became saved. Until now, she had depended on her small network of family and friends

WHO HAD BECOME AWARE OF THE RELATIONSHIP AND ITS DYNAMICS. BUT SHE NOW UNDERSTOOD THAT THIS SITUATION WOULD MOST SURELY REQUIRE A HIGHER POWER AND THE ULTIMATE SOURCE OF STRENGTH TO GET HER THROUGH THIS TIME.

CHAPTER 22

A COVEN OF WITCHES

RICO BECAME ENGULFED IN DEVIL ENERGY. HE COULDN'T FIGURE OUT WHY OR HOW HE KEPT ALLOWING HIS LIFE TO SPIRAL OUT OF CONTROL. HE DIDN'T EVEN RECOGNIZE HIMSELF ANYMORE. HE REFUSED TO STAND IN FRONT OF HIS LARGE MIRROR. ONE DAY, HE CAME HOME EARLY FROM WORK AS A RESULT OF FEELING UNWELL, ONLY TO RECEIVE THE BIGGEST SHOCK OF HIS ENTIRE LIFE! HE THOUGHT HE HEARD VOICES BUT WASN'T EXACTLY SURE WHO WOULD BE HOME AT THIS HOUR BECAUSE HIS KARMIC HOUSEMATE WOULD BE AT WORK DURING THIS TIME OF DAY.

HEARING SOUNDS, RICO QUIETLY FOLLOWED THE VOICES DOWNSTAIRS TO HIS BASEMENT WHERE HE QUIET AS A MOUSE BEGAN TO PEEK IN THE DIRECTION OF THE STRANGE NOISES. AT FIRST IT SOUNDED LIKE A GROUP OF PEOPLE WERE SINGING OR RECITING SOME FORM OF WORDS LIKE IN A THEATER PLAY. SOON HE DISCOVERED HIS HOUSEMATE AND HER FRIENDS IN A CIRCLE WITH ROBES AND HOODS CHANTING SPELLS AND RITUALS. HE COULD HARDLY BELIEVE WHAT HE WAS SEEING AND HEARING, BUT HE FORCED HIMSELF TO REMAIN QUIET AND OBSERVE.

RICO COULD SEE A LARGE CONTAINER OF SOME KIND IN THE MIDDLE OF THE CIRCLE WITH A FIRE CIRCLED AROUND IT. AS THE CHANTING CONTINUED EACH PERSON STEPPED FORWARD ONE BY ONE TO ADD SOMETHING TO THE LARGE BURNING CONTAINER. HE NOW RECOGNIZED THE REST OF THE CIRCLE AS THEY STEPPED FORWARD AND THEIR FACES WERE SHOWN IN THE LIGHT FROM THE FIRE. RICO

CONTINUED TO REMAIN SILENT TRYING TO UNDERSTAND SOME OF THE WORDS THAT WERE BEING CHANTED WHEN THE GROUP SUDDENLY SWITCHED THEIR LANGUAGE TO ENGLISH.

WHAT RICO OBSERVED AND HEARD HAD HIM THOROUGHLY SHAKEN! THEY REPEATED THE CHANTS SEVERAL TIMES EACH CAUSING HIM TO ALMOST TURN AND RUN TO THE BATHROOM AND RELEASE HIS STOMACH'S CONTENTS. THE CHANTS BECAME LOUDER EACH TIME THEY REPEATED IT AND HE COULD SEE ITEMS IN EACH PERSON'S HANDS NOW. THEY CONTINUED TO CHANT "WE OFFER THE SEXUAL DEMON TO YOU RICO" WE OFFER THE SEXUAL DEMON TO YOU RICO" OVER AND OVER THEY CHANTED.

RICO NOTICED THAT HIS KARMIC HOUSEMATE BEGAN TO MAKE GRINDING MOTIONS WITH HER HIPS AND GYRATE HER VAGINA AROUND A PAIR OF HIS UNDERWEAR WHICH HE HADN'T SEEN FOR QUITE SOME

TIME NOW. SHE MIMICKED A SEXUAL ENCOUNTER THAT TURNED OBSCENE AND VULGAR WHILE THE OTHERS URGED HER ON. HE WAS TOTALLY DISGUSTED.

WHEN SHE FINALLY MIMICKED AN ORGASM, SHE RELINQUISHED THE UNDERWEAR TO THE LARGE POT. PANTING AND BREATHING HEAVILY SHE MADE HER WAY BACK TO HER PLACE IN THE CIRCLE. WHAT RICO THOUGHT MIGHT HAVE BEEN THE END OF A SHOCKING AND HARD TRUTH TO HANDLE ONLY CONTINUED TO GET WORSE AS HE SPOTTED SEVERAL PICTURES OF RHEA BEING PASSED FROM ONE OF THE GROUP MEMBERS TO THE NEXT. RICO SAW THE MALE OF THE GROUP, PAUSE TO LOOK AT THE PICTURES OF RHEA AND THEN RUB THEM ALONG HIS PRIVATE PARTS WHILE THE OTHERS CLAPPED, AND CHEERED HIM ON.

THE GROUP BEGAN TO CHANT OVER RHEA'S PICTURE "DIE BITCH DIE" "RHEA WILL DIE!" THEY CHANTED

REPEATEDLY. RICO COULD NOT BARE TO HEAR THOSE WORDS BEING SPOKEN ABOUT THE WOMAN HE STILL LOVED SO HE LEFT THE BASEMENT AND GOT INTO HIS CAR TO GET AS FAR AWAY FROM THE BIZARRE SCENE BEING ACTED OUT IN HIS OWN HOME.

HE TOOK A LONG DRIVE FIRST JUST TO GET SOME AIR AWAY FROM THE AWFUL SCENE HE HAD THE MISFORTUNE TO WITNESS. HE WAS STILL QUITE SHAKEN AND WEAK FROM HIS EARLIER ILLNESS AND SHOULD PROBABLY NOT HAVE DRIVEN ANYWHERE BUT HE COULD NOT ALLOW HIMSELF TO REMAIN INSIDE HIS HOME WITH THAT EVIL GOING ON FOR ANOTHER SECOND. WHEN HE FINALLY STOPPED THE CAR AND LOOKED AT HIS SURROUNDINGS, HE REALIZED THAT HE WAS AT RHEA'S APARTMENT COMPLEX.

HE DIDN'T EVEN REMEMBER CONSCIOUSLY DRIVING THERE YET HERE HE WAS. HE DIDN'T KNOW HOW TO FACE HER OR EVEN HOW TO APPROACH HER AFTER ALL THIS

TIME. HE SIMPLY SAT THERE AND WENT OVER THE EVENTS OF THIS DAY FROM START UNTIL NOW. HE MADE A MENTAL NOTE OF THE PEOPLE AND ALL THE THINGS THAT WERE BEING DONE AND SAID WHILE HE OBSERVED THEM UNNOTICED. HE REALLY DIDN'T KNOW WHO THIS WOMAN WAS HE HAD BEEN BUILDING A LIFE WITH AND SHARING A HOME WITH ALL THIS TIME. HOW COULD HE HAVE BEEN SO BLIND? HOW COME HE NEVER SAW ANY CLUES TO THIS SITUATION BEFORE NOW?

CHAPTER 23

GRAVEYARD RITUALS

Rico decided to leave and return home to see if the coven had dispersed and gone their separate ways yet. He decided to drive past his home first to see what everything looked like from the street view. Just as he was about to drive past, he saw his Karmic housemate drive away after tossing something into the backseat of her vehicle. He decided to play detective and follow her unnoticed to see what she was up to now.

Rico followed her to a nearby cemetery where she drove

AROUND UNTIL SHE SAW A FRESHLY DUG GRAVE. HE SAW HER RETRIEVE THE ITEM FROM THE BACKSEAT OF THE CAR AND TAKE IT TO THE SITE. SHE LOOKED AROUND TO MAKE SURE NONE OF THE CARETAKERS OR GROUNDSKEEPERS WERE AROUND TO WITNESS HER PRESENCE.

RICO COULD BARELY MAKE OUT THE ITEM IN HER HAND, BUT HE RECOGNIZED A PIECE OF CLOTH THAT WAS FAMILIAR TO HIM. IT WAS TAKEN FROM AN OVERSIZED TEE-SHIRT THAT HE HAD GOTTEN FROM RHEA'S CLOSET ONE DAY WHEN HE'D BEEN CAUGHT IN THE RAIN. WRAPPED INSIDE OF THE CUT MATERIAL WAS A DOLL THAT WAS SUPPOSED TO BE A LIKENESS TO HIS LADY LOVE! WHEN RICO SAW THIS, HE NEARLY LOST IT. IT TOOK EVERY BIT OF STRENGTH NOT TO RUSH UP BEHIND HER AND PUSH HER INSIDE. "GOD HELP ME," HE WHISPERED TO HIMSELF BEFORE GETTING INTO HIS CAR QUICKLY AND MAKING HIS WAY BACK HOME.

RICO COULD FEEL DEEP DOWN IN THE PIT OF HIS STOMACH THAT NOTHING WOULD EVER BE THE SAME BETWEEN HIM AND THIS WOMAN AGAIN. HE SOON BEGAN TO REALIZE THAT FOR THE FIRST TIME IN HIS LIFE HE KNEW WHAT IT FELT LIKE TO HATE ANOTHER HUMAN BEING AND THAT WAS A FEELING HE NEVER WANTED TO HAVE. HE KNEW HE NEEDED TO SEEK A HIGHER POWER AND SPEND SOME TIME IN PRAYER ABOUT THIS ENTIRE SITUATION BECAUSE INSTINCTIVELY HE COULD FEEL THAT ONLY GOD COULD HELP HIM NOW.

CHAPTER 24

PLAYING THE LONG GAME

RICO THOUGHT LONG AND HARD ABOUT WHETHER TO CONFRONT HIS KARMIC HOUSEMATE OR TO JUST WAIT AND WATCH TO SEE WHAT ELSE HE COULD DISCOVER ABOUT THIS HIDDEN DARK LIFESTYLE SHE SO OBVIOUSLY PARTICIPATED IN. HE FOUND HIMSELF RELIVING THE SCENE REPEATEDLY IN HIS MIND UNTIL HE THOUGHT HE WOULD EXPLODE. HE KNEW HE HAD TO GET A GRIP ON THIS AND GET OUT OF HIS HEAD BECAUSE IT WOULDN'T DO ANYONE ANY GOOD TO MAKE HIMSELF SICK.

LATELY, HE'D BEEN EXPERIENCING MIGRAINE HEADACHES ON A REGULAR BASIS, BUT HE FELT IT WAS BECAUSE HE WAS TIRED FROM BEING OVERWORKED AND LYING AWAKE AT NIGHT THINKING TOO MUCH. HE ADMITTED TO HIMSELF THAT HE WAS INDEED WORRIED ABOUT RHEA AND WHAT THIS MEANT FOR HER? HE VOWED TO WATCH HER AND KEEP HER SAFE 24/7 IF HE HAD TO. AND HEAVEN HELP THE PERSON WHO WOULD TRY TO HARM HER BECAUSE HE KNEW HE WOULD GO TO THE EXTREME TO PROTECT HER.

RHEA SAT DOWN ON A PARK BENCH TAKING A SMALL BREAK FROM HER WALKING TRAIL. SHE PARTICULARLY LIKED THIS PARK FOR EXERCISE BECAUSE THE FACILITIES WERE CLEAN, AND THE PARK WAS NICE AND WELL MANAGED. HER THOUGHTS WENT TO RICO AS THEY SO OFTEN DID DURING THE DAY. HE WOULD CALL AND CHECK UP ON HER AT LEAST, 3-4 TIMES A WEEK AND STOP BY TO SEE HER A FEW TIMES ALSO.

HE HAD BECOME MORE LIKE THE OLD RICO SHE FIRST DATED BEFORE THINGS WENT SOUTH FOR THE CONNECTION. LATELY SHE BEGAN TO FEEL AS IF SHE WERE BEING WATCHED OR FOLLOWED, BUT SHE DECIDED TO FOLLOW HER USUAL ROUTINE ANYWAY AND PAY CLOSER ATTENTION TO SEE IF MAYBE IT WAS JUST HER IMAGINATION, AND NO DANGER WAS ANYWHERE AROUND HER.

ONE DAY RHEA WENT SHOPPING AT SOME OF HER FAVORITE OUTLETS AND NOTICED A CAR THAT SEEMED TO TURN UP AT EVERY STORE SHE STOPPED AT. THE WINDOWS HAD HEAVY TINT IN THEM SO SHE COULDN'T MAKE OUT WHO WAS INSIDE. HAVING BEEN STALKED BY AN EX- HUSBAND IN THE PAST SHE IMMEDIATELY PUT HER GUARD UP AND DECIDED TO CUT SHOPPING SHORT FOR THE DAY AND HEAD HOME. SURE ENOUGH, THE CAR WAS TRAILING HER TRYING TO KEEP A LARGE ENOUGH DISTANCE TO NOT BE DISCOVERED.

WHEN SHE GOT INSIDE AND SECURED THE DOORS AND WINDOWS, SHE CALLED RICO AND ASKED HIM TO COME OVER. WHEN RICO GOT THERE, SHE EXPLAINED ABOUT THE CAR THAT FOLLOWED HER ON HER SHOPPING TRIPS AND ABOUT THE EERIE FEELING SHE HAD AT THE PARK.

TO HER SURPRISE, RICO IMMEDIATELY TOOK OFF OUT THE DOOR AFTER A QUICK GOODBYE KISS. HIS ONLY WORDS WERE, "I'LL SEE YOU LATER" LEAVING A PUZZLED RHEA LEFT TO WONDER EXACTLY WHAT THE HELL WAS GOING ON?

WHEN THE TWINS MET UP AGAIN RHEA COULD SENSE THAT SOMETHING HAD HAPPENED WHICH MADE RICO APPEAR TO BE ON EDGE. HE ASKED HER MORE THAN ONCE IF SHE WERE FEELING OKAY AND LOOKED HER UP AND DOWN AS IF HE WERE AN EMERGENCY ROOM PHYSICIAN TRYING TO MAKE A MEDICAL DIAGNOSIS.

THIS HOWEVER MADE HER FEEL A LITTLE UNEASY AND MORE THAN ONCE SHE CHECKED HERSELF IN THE LARGE MIRROR OF HER BEDROOM TO SEE IF SHE WERE PALE OR SICK LOOKING OR IF THERE WERE SOMETHING ABOUT HER APPEARANCE THAT SHE SHOULD BE CONCERNED ABOUT. WHEN SHE WAS SATISFIED THAT HER SKIN-TONE SEEMED HEALTHY ENOUGH SHE JOINED RICO IN THE SITTING ROOM TO SEE IF HE WOULD LET HER IN ON WHAT EXACTLY HAD HIM SO FILLED WITH ANXIETY REGARDING HER APPEARANCE.

RICO TALKED AROUND ANY QUESTIONS RHEA ASKED IGNORING THEM ALTOGETHER FOR A MORE PLAYFUL AND JOVIAL PERSONALITY WHICH WAS IN DIRECT CONTRAST TO THE ONE HE'D DISPLAYED ON HIS LAST VISIT. SHE COULDN'T QUITE MAKE OUT WHAT THIS ALL MEANT, AND SHE WAS TOTALLY IN THE DARK AS TO WHY HIS PERSONALITY SEEMED TO SHIFT AND CHANGE FROM DAY TO DAY. SHE FINALLY STOPPED STRESSING OVER

IT AND DECIDED TO JUST WATCH TO SEE WHERE IT WOULD ALL LEAD.

IN THE DAYS THAT FOLLOWED, RICO TOOK TIME TO CALL AND CHECK ON RHEA. BUT INSTEAD OF VISIBLY HOVERING, HE WATCHED AND MONITORED HER FROM A DISTANCE. RHEA REMAINED IN A STATE OF CONFUSION AND TO MAKE MATTERS WORSE, SHE BEGAN TO FEEL ILL, AND SYMPTOMS BECAME EVIDENT THAT SOMETHING WAS INDEED WRONG WITH HER BODY. LITTLE DID SHE KNOW THAT SHE WOULD SOON GET THE SHOCK OF HER LIFE AND A CONFIRMATION ABOUT HERSELF THAT SHE COULD NEVER HAVE EXPECTED OR ANTICIPATED.

CHAPTER 25

SURPRISE

The next few nights, Rhea tossed and turned feeling hot and achy in certain parts of her body she hadn't felt since she was a young woman. Her breasts were hot, swollen, and achy. She finally got a few hours rest after placing cold packs on her breasts and a heating pad on her back. She knew she needed to see a doctor as soon as possible and would make an appointment right away to get to the bottom of this situation.

When Rico called the next morning, Rhea was crying from

THE PAIN SHE WAS IN. RICO ASKED WHAT WAS WRONG AND WOULDN'T ALLOW HER TO DISMISS HIS CONCERN WITHOUT A DEFINITIVE ANSWER. SHE CAREFULLY EXPLAINED HER SYMPTOMS TO HIM AND STARTLED HERSELF TO HEAR THEM SPOKEN ALOUD. SHE THOUGHT SHE MUST HAVE SURELY BEEN IN DENIAL ABOUT WHAT ALL OF THIS MEANT.

SHE EXPLAINED THE ACHY BREASTS, BACKACHE, NAUSEA TO THE POINT OF LOST APPETITE. RICO LISTENED TO THE SYMPTOMS CAREFULLY THEN ASKED WITHOUT HESITATION, "ARE YOU PREGNANT?" RHEA HAD TO PAUSE FOR A FEW MOMENTS BEFORE SHE COULD GIVE AN ANSWER TO A QUESTION THAT NEVER EVEN OCCURRED TO HER. SHE ANSWERED AS TRUTHFUL AS SHE COULD, "I DON'T KNOW BUT I INTEND TO FIND OUT."

RHEA MADE AN APPOINTMENT TO SEE HER OB/GYN DOCTOR WHEN AN APPOINTMENT WAS AVAILABLE BUT UNFORTUNATELY, SHE BEGAN

BLEEDING QUITE HEAVILY BEFORE IT CAME UP AND HAD TO BE SEEN RIGHT AWAY ON AN EMERGENCY BASIS. AFTER SEVERAL TESTS WERE MADE AND REVIEWED, RHEA WENT HOME AND STAYED IN BED TRYING TO RECOVER FOR SEVERAL DAYS. SHE COULD NEVER HAVE IMAGINED IN HER WILDEST DREAMS THAT HER BODY COULD OR WOULD HAVE BETRAYED HER IN THE FORM OF NATURE TAKING A TURN IN AN UNEXPECTED DIRECTION.

BUT HERE IT WAS, AND SHE WAS FACED WITH THE FACT THAT THIS WAS A LOSS SHE HAD TO RECONCILE WITH, WITHOUT EVEN GETTING A CHANCE TO PROCESS WHAT IT ALL MEANT. THE ONLY THING SHE REALIZED WAS THAT MOTHER NATURE HAD GIVEN HER A GREAT BIG SHOCK WITH THIS ONE AND SHE NEEDED TO LEARN TO TAKE PRECAUTIONS SO THAT THIS NEVER HAPPENED AGAIN.

CHAPTER 26

HEALING AFTER A GREAT LOSS

During the next several weeks and months, Rhea felt as if she'd stepped out of her life and into a parallel universe or something from a Stephen King movie. She took the time she needed to heal her body and now it was time to figure out exactly what was going on with Rico. During this whole ordeal he became very quiet, withdrawn, and quite reclusive.

Rico checked up on her every morning and sometimes during the day with phone calls mostly.

Rhea couldn't figure out why he stayed away during her recovery. Where was the loving attentive man that was usually by her side? Why didn't he realize that she needed him now more than ever as she mourned the loss of their baby?

Surely, he must've been as surprised as she to learn of this special gift that could have only been sent from God. Finally, she received what Oprah refers to as the "ah ha moment." Rhea knew as a trained counselor and therapist that everyone processes grief and loss in their own way.

So, she simply placed her thoughts on her healing and knew instinctively that Rico must be doing the same. As she rested and worked towards her recovery, Rhea had the chance to study long and hard information about what to expect from a

Divine Counterpart during a Twin Flame Union.

What Rhea discovered about Twin Flames had her concerned, but it did answer some of the questions that had kept her up at night wondering how this story was supposed to play out and when would Rico become Divinely Guided down the path, he was meant to walk on beside her?

She began to understand why his actions were hot and cold and in and out most of the time. She now understood why the traits he displayed were simply not those of a Divine Being and most certainly not a Divine Masculine who like herself, was sent directly into this life so that the two of them could fulfill a Divine Mission together during this lifetime.

Rhea read about the dark night of the soul that counterparts must

TRANSITION THROUGH TO BECOME THEIR HIGHEST SELVES BY KILLING AND DESTROYING THEN SHEDDING THE EGO WHICH IS WHAT STIFLES GROWTH AND HINDERS ABUNDANCE AND PROSPERITY AS WELL AS ASCENDING TO THE HIGHEST LEVEL OF GROWTH ONE CAN OBTAIN. WHEN RHEA HAD FINISHED READING EVERYTHING AND ANYTHING SHE COULD GET HER HANDS ON REGARDING THE TWIN FLAME JOURNEY, SHE KNEW WITHOUT THE TINIEST BIT OF DOUBT THAT IF SHE AND RICO WERE EVER TO COME TOGETHER AS GOD HAD ORDAINED THEM TO, SHE WOULD HAVE TO TALK WITH HIM AND EXPLAIN THE THINGS SHE'D LEARNED TO HIM SO THAT HE COULD RELEASE HIS TOXIC STREET WAYS ONCE AND FOR ALL BEFORE GOD STEPS IN AND SENDS KARMA HIS WAY TO DIRECT HIM TO HIS RIGHTFUL PLACE THE HARD WAY.

CHAPTER 27

RUMORS/THE LYIN-KING

WHAT CAME NEXT WAS VERY UNEXPECTED AND SAD. SAD BECAUSE SHE KNEW THAT WHATEVER EVIL AND DEMONIC ENTITY HAD ATTACHED ITSELF TO THE MAN, SHE USED TO KNOW AND LOVE, HAD NOW CONSUMED HIM TOTALLY. THE STREETS WERE TALKING ABOUT HIS CHANGES AND EVEN PEOPLE HE HAD KNOWN ALL HIS LIFE COULDN'T BELIEVE HOW DIFFERENT HE WAS OR WHAT THEY WERE HEARING. THE MAN THEY KNEW HIM TO BE WAS A RESPECTFUL FATHER AND PERFORMER IN THE COMMUNITY.

THE RUMOR MILL WAS CONSTANTLY GRINDING, AND THE RUMORS WERE

BEYOND BIZARRE AND CRAZY. SOME WERE ABOUT HER AND OTHERS WERE ABOUT ALL THE OTHER WOMEN HE HAD ALLEGEDLY BECOME INVOLVED WITH INCLUDING HIS KARMIC HOUSEMATE AND ALL THE OTHER KARMEESHAS' IN HIS LITTLE HAREM.

MOST OF THE RUMORS THAT GOT BACK TO RHEA CONCERNING HER RELATIONSHIP WITH THE MAN WHO CLAIMED TO LOVE HER WERE VERY DISRESPECTFUL AND HURTFUL. SHE WAS TOLD THAT BEHIND HER BACK HE WOULD TALK TRASH ABOUT HER CLAIMING HER TO HAVE MENTAL INSTABILITY SUCH AS BIPOLAR OR SCHIZOPHRENIA AND THAT SHE WAS NOTHING BUT A DRAMA QUEEN WHO STRESSED HIM OUT AND CAUSED HIM ANXIETY. HE ACCUSED HER A BEING A WITCH AND SAID SHE'D PROBABLY PUT A SEX SPELL ON HIM WHICH KEPT HIM COMING BACK TO BE INTIMATE WITH HER.

WHEN RHEA HEARD THESE RUMORS, SHE BECAME SO ANGRY SHE

CONFRONTED HIM ABOUT THEM BUT OF COURSE HE DENIED THEM ALL. SHE TOLD HIM THAT THE STREETS WERE TALKING ABOUT HIM AND SAYING HOW HE HAD BECOME SEXUALLY PROMISCUOUS WITH YOUNG WOMEN AND GIRLS AND EVEN WOMEN WHO WERE SEX WORKERS STRIPPERS AND LADIES OF THE NIGHT. SHE ASKED HIM HOW HE COULD GIVE HIS TIME AND ENERGY TO SOMEONE WHO WAS A STRICTLY "LAY FOR PAY?" BUT AS USUAL, HE DENIED THE ACCUSATIONS AND DISMISSED THE CONVERSATION SAYING HE DIDN'T DO DRAMA.

HOWEVER, SHE ALSO INFORMED HIM THAT AS THE RUMOR MILL CONTINUED TO TICK, SHE ALSO HEARD THAT HE HAD BECOME SO ENGROSSED IN THIS TOXIC STREET LIFE THAT HE WAS ALLOWING ALL MORALS AND VALUES TO BE IGNORED FOR A LIFESTYLE FILLED WITH THREESOMES, ORGIES, SEX PARTIES, INCLUDING A TRANSGENDER ASSOCIATE FROM THE LGBT COMMUNITY!

ALTHOUGH, RHEA HAD NO PROBLEMS WITH THE INFORMATION, AND HAD FRIENDS FROM THE COMMUNITY HERSELF, SHE DID FEEL THAT IF THERE WERE INTIMACIES BEING CONDUCTED BETWEEN HIM AND A SAME PARTY SEX PARTNER, SHE SHOULD HAVE BEEN INFORMED ABOUT THAT CONSIDERING THE FACT THAT SHE WAS STILL INVOLVED PHYSICALLY WITH THIS MAN. HE WAS SOMEONE WHO HAD BECOME ALMOST A STRANGER TO HER NOW. RHEA WAS MORTIFIED AND COULDN'T BELIEVE THIS WAS THE SAME PERSON WHOM SHE THOUGHT SHE WOULD EVENTUALLY BUILD A LIFE WITH AND BLEND FAMILIES WITH.

THE MAN WHO HAD SO INTIMATELY MADE SUCH SWEET LOVE TO HER ON NUMEROUS OCCASIONS. THE MAN WHOM SHE HAD SHARED THE LOSS OF A CHILD WITH. HER MAN! OR WAS IT ALL JUST AN ILLUSION BEHIND THE MASK HE WORE? HAD HE ALWAYS HIDDEN THE TRUE RICO? OR WAS THIS THE ONE HE CONSTANTLY DISPLAYED FOR POLITE SOCIETY?

ONLY TIME WOULD TELL, AND RHEA KNEW INSTINCTIVELY THAT THIS MATTER WAS UNDER DIVINE TIMING AND GOD WOULD BE THE ONE WHO WOULD REVEAL THE TRUTH WHEN HE WAS READY.

CHAPTER 28

SLEEPING WITH
THE DEVIL

During the next year, Rhea found herself in a series of events that made her feel as if she lived in an alternate reality instead of in her own world. The relationship between her and Rico became more bizarre by the day. So much so, she felt that it was time to investigate and do her research to find out what was really going on with this situation. Before she could make plans regarding the situation, Rico's erratic behavior became even more aggressive with her than usual. She had no clue

WHO HE WAS ANYMORE OR WHY HE SEEMED SO ANGRY WITH HER.

RHEA DECIDED IT WAS TIME TO DO MORE RESEARCH ON THIS SITUATION AND TO LEAN ON THE KNOWLEDGE SHE'D ACQUIRED AT THE UNIVERSITY IN PSYCHOLOGY WHICH WAS VERY FAMILIAR TO HER. SHE BEGAN TO JOURNAL RICO'S BEHAVIOR AND OUTBURSTS AS SHE WAS TAUGHT TO DO WHILE STUDYING FOR HER DEGREES.

BUT, AS TIME PROGRESSED, SHE BEGAN TO FEEL AS IF THE MAN SHE LOVED AND RESPECTED NO LONGER EXISTED AND SHE FOUND HERSELF TELLING HIM SEVERAL TIMES THROUGHOUT THE YEAR TO GO AWAY AND LEAVE HER ALONE. THE REACTION SHE GOT FROM HIM AFTER HEARING THE REJECTIONS ONLY ANGERED HIM MORE AND AS A RESULT, HE BEGAN TO FORCE HER TO BE INTIMATE WITH HIM AND STRONG ARMED HER INTO SUBMISSION WHEN SHE FOUGHT BACK.

RHEA KNEW SHE HAD TO DO SOMETHING QUICKLY BEFORE SHE GOT HURT SO SHE INVITED ONE OF HER CLOSEST AND OLDEST FRIENDS OVER AND EXPLAINED EVERYTHING TO HER OVER A BOTTLE OF WINE JUST IN CASE SOMETHING SINISTER WERE TO HAPPEN BETWEEN HER AND RICO. HER FRIEND LISTENED CLOSELY TO HER WITH A SYMPATHETIC EAR. BOTH WOMEN LOOKED AT THE JOURNAL NOTES AND SAID AT THE SAME TIME "THIS IS A NARCISSIST." THE REALIZATION HIT RHEA LIKE A SLEDGEHAMMER.

RHEA KNEW THE SIGNS AND SYMPTOMS OF NARCISSISM. BUT IT WASN'T SOMETHING SHE'D EVER ENCOUNTERED IN A RELATIONSHIP SINCE HER TEEN YEARS AND IT CAME AS A SURPRISE NOW. SHE HAD TO ADMIT ALL THE CLASSIC BEHAVIORS THAT CAME WITH THIS DISORDER WERE INDEED PRESENT IN RICO. RHEA TOLD HER FRIEND ABOUT ALL THE RUMORS THAT HAD BEEN CIRCULATING ABOUT HIM AND ADMITTED FOR THE FIRST

TIME OUT LOUD THAT SHE WOULDN'T BE SURPRISED IF ONE OR MORE OF THEM WERE TRUE.

WHEN RHEA TOLD TRACIE ABOUT THE PLAN, SHE'D MADE TO GET TO THE BOTTOM OF THIS, TRACIE AGREED SHE HAD TO DO SOMETHING, AND THAT SHE WOULD HELP IF SHE COULD. SHE ALSO REMINDED RHEA THAT SHE TOLD HER TO BE CAREFUL WITH RICO FROM THE VERY BEGINNING ALTHOUGH SHE COULDN'T FIGURE A REASON WHY SHE HAD WARNED HER FRIEND, BUT NOW SHE KNEW.

ONE DAY RICO CAME OVER IN A PARTICULARLY FRISKY MOOD WANTING TO SPEND SOME INTIMATE TIME WITH HER. HE SEEMED MORE LIKE THE OLD RICO WHICH MADE HER HAPPY TO SPEND SOME QUALITY TIME WITH HIM AND RESUME THEIR REGULAR LOVEMAKING ROUTINE WITHOUT ALL THE DRAMA AND AGGRESSION.

RICO WAS PASSIONATE AND ATTENTIVE TO HER BODY AND RHEA BEGAN

TO RELAX AND ENJOY HERSELF. SUDDENLY, RICO EXITED HER LADY PART AND ENTERED HER IN A PLACE THAT HAD NEVER BEEN TOUCHED BY A MAN BEFORE, AT LEAST NONE OTHER THAN HER DOCTOR. HER INSTINCT WAS TO FIGHT BUT HE HAD HER PINNED UNDER HIM AND SHE COULDN'T MOVE A MUSCLE. HE BEGAN TO WHISPER TENDER WORDS TO HER ASKING HER TO RELAX AND ALLOW HIM TO MAKE LOVE TO HER BECAUSE HE PROMISED NOT TO HURT HER.

AT THIS POINT, THERE WAS NOTHING SHE COULD DO TO MOVE ANYWAY, SO SHE RELAXED UNTIL IT WAS FINISHED. ALTHOUGH SHE DIDN'T THINK SHE'D REALLY ENJOY IT, HE WAS TRUE TO HIS WORD BECAUSE HE DID NOT HURT HER THIS TIME. HE HAD SIMPLY CAUGHT HER OFF GUARD.

HOWEVER, THE NEXT TIME HE TRIED IT HE HAD HER STANDING UP AND THAT WAS NOT PLEASANT AT ALL. HE COULD SOMEHOW SENSE SHE WAS UNCOMFORTABLE AND ASKED IF SHE

WANTED HIM TO STOP. SHE TOLD HIM SHE DIDN'T LIKE IT THIS WAY AND HE STOPPED IMMEDIATELY.

AFTER THAT ENCOUNTER, HE DIDN'T TRY AGAIN WHICH WAS FINE WITH HER BECAUSE AT THIS POINT, SHE NEEDED TO FIGURE OUT A WAY FOR BOTH PARTIES TO ENJOY THIS NEWEST VERSION OF THEIR INTIMATE ENCOUNTERS IF THIS WAS TO BE PART OF THEIR ROUTINE ON A CONSISTENT BASIS. ALTHOUGH IT WAS NEW TO HER, SHE HAD A FEELING THAT THIS WAS SOMETHING HE MORE THAN LIKELY EXPERIENCED IN OTHER RELATIONSHIPS AND WANTED TO SHARE THE EXPERIENCE WITH HER ALSO.

CHAPTER 29

SEARCHING FOR ANSWERS,

Rhea replayed that night repeatedly in her head feeling as if something was truly wrong with Rico based on his passive-aggressive behavior and the fact that he'd become so aggressive towards her. She continued to journal their encounters but felt that this method wasn't enough to help her with the behavior that had spiraled out of control so abruptly. It was time to take matters into her own hands to find out the answers she so desperately needed.

THE NEXT TIME RICO MADE AN APPEARANCE SHE DECIDED TO TRY AND HAVE A HEART-TO-HEART CONVERSATION WITH HIM TO VOICE SOME OF THE CONCERNS SHE FELT ABOUT HIS BEHAVIOR TOWARDS HER AND TO HEAR HIS REASONING BEHIND THE CHANGES WHICH SEEMED TO AFFECT THEIR LIVES SO COMPLETELY.

RHEA OFFERED RICO TO SPEAK FIRST BUT AS USUAL HE DECLINED SO SHE BEGAN TELLING HIM ABOUT THE THINGS THAT WERE CONCERNING HER AND AFFECTING THEIR UNION. SHE EXPLAINED SLOWLY AND QUIETLY WITHOUT SHOWING SIGNS OF MALICE OR ANGER SO THAT HE WOULDN'T FEEL VERBALLY ATTACKED OR COMBATIVE.

BUT IT WAS NO USE, BECAUSE NO MATTER HOW TACTFUL AND CONSIDERATE FOR HIS FEELINGS HER WORDS WERE SPOKEN, HE STILL BECAME ANGRY AND YELLED AT HER BEFORE STORMING OUT AND SLAMMING THE DOOR ON HER WHILE

She was still asking him, what was wrong? He showed total disregard for her concerns and acted downright ignorant and emotionally immature in her opinion. For Rhea, this was the final straw.

Full of anger and hurt, she grabbed car keys and followed him. She skillfully navigated her Chrysler 300 at a safe distance behind his Jeep so she wouldn't be detected. Rhea was so hurt by Rico's words and actions she found herself fighting a losing battle to hold back the tears that were spilling making it difficult to see while driving.

Finally, Rico stopped and parked his truck in a driveway at what she assumed was his home. Rhea knew this would be a long night so she found her own parking spot down the street which was shielded by trees so she wouldn't be seen by the occupants of the

HOUSE SHE WOULD BE TARGETING. RHEA MADE HERSELF COMFORTABLE IN HER CAR AND PULLED OUT SOME OF HER AND RICO'S FAVORITE OLDIES ON CD'S.

RHEA NOTICED THAT PARKED WHERE SHE WAS CURRENTLY, SHE HAD A BIRD'S EYE VIEW OF RICO AND HIS KARMIC HOUSEMATE'S HOME. BRIEFLY, SHE FOUND HER MIND CONJURING PICTURES OF HIM WITH THE KARMIC LIVING AS A COUPLE AND DOING THINGS THAT COUPLES DO LIKE SHARING MEALS AND GROOMING THEMSELVES IN THE SAME BATHROOM WHILE GETTING THEIR DAY STARTED. SHE IMAGINED HIM WALKING HIS BIG BEAUTIFUL SIBERIAN HUSKY AROUND THE YARD PLAYING DOGGY GAMES WHILE THE KARMIC WATCHED OR PREPARED THE EVENING MEAL.

FINALLY, HER MIND WENT WHERE SHE SHOULD NEVER HAVE ALLOWED TO GO. AS SOON SHE IMAGINED THE TWO OF THEM SLEEPING TOGETHER IN BED ALL NESTLED TOGETHER FOR

THE NIGHT, SHE WILLED HER MIND TO STOP. SHE FORCED HER MIND TO STOP RIGHT THERE! THAT WAS ENOUGH OF THAT! SHE CHANGED THE MUSIC TO SMOOTH JAZZ AND TRIED TO RELAX UNTIL IT WAS TIME TO MAKE HER MOVE.

AS DUSK TURNED INTO NIGHTFALL, RHEA BEGAN TO NOTICE ALL THE CARS THAT WERE SHOWING UP AT RICO'S HOME. SOME WERE IN THE DRIVEWAY DIRECTLY ALONGSIDE HIS AND AS THEY CONTINUED TO ARRIVE, SOME PARKED DIRECTLY IN FRONT OF THE HOUSE PARALLEL WITH THE CURB SIMILAR TO THE WAY SHE HAD PARKED ON THE OPPOSITE SIDE OF THE STREET DOWN FURTHER TOWARD THE MIDDLE OF THE BLOCK. SHE BEGAN TO WONDER IF THEY WERE HAVING A HOUSE PARTY OR GET TOGETHER OF SOME KIND? OF ALL THE NIGHTS TO PLAN A HOME INVASION SHE HAD TO CHOOSE ONE WHERE THERE WOULD BE HOUSEGUESTS SHE THOUGHT?

RHEA'S SUPERPOWER INTUITION TOLD HER TO STAY PUT WHEN SHE THOUGHT ABOUT ABANDONING THE WHOLE PLAN AND TRYING FOR ANOTHER DAY. BUT SOMETHING SEEMED OFF. IF THERE WERE A HOUSE PARTY HAPPENING, WHERE WAS THE MUSIC? SHOULDN'T SHE HEAR VOICES AT LEAST? SHE COUNTED AT LEAST FIVE CARS EXCLUDING RICO'S AND AT LEAST TWO PEOPLE HAD SHARED A RIDE.

RHEA DECIDED TO WAIT UNTIL EVERYONE ARRIVED TO FIGURE OUT IF IT WERE SAFE TO CONTINUE WITH HER PLANS. AS TIME WENT ON, RHEA BEGAN TO NOTICE THAT THE HOUSE NOT ONLY REMAINED QUIET, BUT IT ALSO SEEMED VERY DARK WITH ONLY AN OUTSIDE LIGHT FOR SAFETY. THIS SEEMED VERY SUSPICIOUS.

SO, THROWING CAUTION TO THE WIND, RHEA DECIDED TO WALK AROUND TO THE BACK OF THE HOUSE TO SEE IF THE PARTY WAS IN THE BACK YARD. AGAIN, RHEA WAS SHOCKED TO FIND

THAT THE BACK OF THE HOUSE WAS EVEN MORE QUIET AND DARK THAN THE FRONT. SHE WAS BAFFLED AT THIS DISCOVERY BUT MORE CURIOUS ABOUT WHAT WAS REALLY HAPPENING, SO SHE FORGED AHEAD WITH HER PLANS.

CHAPTER 30

A SHOCKING DISCOVERY

Rhea moved around the outside of the house casing it like a professional cat burglar. Rhea tried several of the windows and doors to see if any were left open for easy access. Finally, she found that one of the block windows in the basement was open and she could wedge herself inside. She tried as hard as she could not to make a sound even though it was a very tight squeeze. She ripped her jeans on a loose nail as she shimmied her way inside the small window.

Once inside, Rhea paused to get her bearings in the dark unfamiliar basement. She carefully moved around wondering where everyone could possibly be. As she became closer to the bottom of the stairs, she thought she heard a noise.

Voices singing she wondered. But this wasn't like any song she'd ever heard. She then saw a locked door that looked very heavy and old where the voices seemed to be coming from. Rhea's logical brain thought that Rico and his band members must be practicing in there where they wouldn't be disturbing his neighbors with their music.

Rhea soon discovered she could not have been further from the truth. She leaned down looking for the doors entry knob but found only a skeleton key. She gently and quietly removed the

KEY FROM THE LOCK AND PEEKED INSIDE. SHE WAS SURPRISED AT HOW MUCH SHE COULD SEE THROUGH THE HOLE BUT EVEN MORE SURPRISED AT THE SIGHT! RHEA SAW PEOPLE IN A CIRCLE WITH FIRE TORCHES AND WHAT LOOKED LIKE PICTURES AND LANTERNS WITH A DOLL THAT RESEMBLED HER ATTACHED. SHE SAW AMULETS AND A FEW BABY ANIMALS RUNNING AROUND THE ROOM. AS SHE FOCUSED IN ON THE SOUNDS COMING FROM THE ROOM, SHE COULDN'T BELIEVE HER EARS. SHE HEARD WHAT THE GROUP WAS CHANTING "DIE BITCH DIE! RHEA WILL DIE!

AT THE SOUND OF THOSE WORDS RHEA KNEW SHE WASN'T SAFE HERE AND THAT SHE NEEDED TO RUN AWAY TO SAFETY AS FAST AS SHE COULD. AS SHE TURNED TO MAKE HER WAY BACK THROUGH THE BASEMENT ENTRANCE WHERE SHE CAME IN, SHE STUMBLED AND KNOCKED OVER THE DOG'S LARGE FEEDING BOWL. IMMEDIATELY THE CHANTING STOPPED.

WITH LIGHTNING SPEED, SHE TOOK OFF FINDING HER WAY TO THE WINDOW AND PRAYING SHE COULD CLIMB THROUGH IT ON TIME. HALFWAY THROUGH THE ENTRANCE OF THE WINDOW, SHE COULD HEAR THE LOUD SQUEAK OF THE OLD DOOR AND FOOTSTEPS AS SHE JUMPED DOWN AND RAN AS FAST AS SHE COULD TO HER CAR.

AS RHEA STARTED HER ENGINE AND PREPARED TO ACCELERATE, SHE LOOKED UP TO SEE ONE OF THE PEOPLE FROM THE COVEN TAKE OFF THE HOOD AND CAPE AND GET INTO RICO'S CAR! NO MISTAKEN HIS FACE AND BUILD IT WAS INDEED RICO! RHEA SCREAMED HYSTERICALLY, CRYING OUT UNCONTROLLABLY UNBELIEVING WHAT HER EYES WERE SEEING.

BUT NO MATTER HOW HER BRAIN WANTED TO DENY IT, HER EYES WERE CLEARLY SEEING HIM TAKE OFF THE ROBE AND LEAVE HIS STREET CLOTHES ON THAT WERE UNDERNEATH THE HOODED ROBE. RHEA SPED AWAY

BACKING THE CHRYSLER ALL THE WAY DOWN THE OPPOSITE SIDE OF THE STREET UNTIL SHE COULD TURN AROUND AND GO FORWARD SAFELY.

CHAPTER 31

CONFRONTATION

Rhea drove as fast as she could still not knowing if Rico had spotted her car and followed her or not. At this point, she had no direction she was just driving to get as far away as she could. Suddenly, she found herself pulling into the parking structure of Tripsy's Lounge. She knew she would be safe here because Johnnie Harris would be here working Security for the owner.

True enough, she saw Johnnie and ran straight into his arms still crying uncontrollably.

SEEING THE STATE RHEA WAS IN, JOHNNIE IMMEDIATELY WENT INTO ACTION TRYING TO CALM HER DOWN LONG ENOUGH TO FIND ANSWERS AS TO WHAT HAPPENED THAT HAD HER SO HYSTERICAL.

TRUTH BE TOLD, SEEING RHEA IN THIS STATE HAD HIM SHAKEN UP A LITTLE ALSO. ONCE IN HIS ARMS, JOHNNIE COULD FEEL HER WHOLE BODY TREMBLING AS IF SHE'D BEEN FRIGHTENED ALMOST TO DEATH. EVEN THOUGH RHEA NEVER DRANK ANYTHING OTHER THAN WATER AND JUICE HE HANDED HER A GLASS OF BRANDY TO SIP. HE KNEW SHE NEEDED IT.

AS SOON AS SHE BEGAN QUIETING DOWN A LITTLE, RICO WALKED IN. HE CAME TOWARD JOHNNIE AND RHEA, BUT JOHNNIE COULD SEE HER VISIBLY GET UPSET AGAIN. AT THAT POINT, JOHNNIE STEPPED IN FRONT OF RHEA AND TOLD RICO TO STEP BACK. RICO IN HIS FEELINGS IMMEDIATELY BECAME AGITATED WITH JOHNNIE'S

INTERFERENCE BUT NEITHER MAN WAS BACKING DOWN. RHEA COULD FEEL THE TENSION BEGINNING TO MOUNT AND KNEW THAT SOMETHING NEEDED TO BE DONE TO STOP THIS CONFRONTATION BEFORE IT WENT TOO FAR.

AT THAT MOMENT, JOHNNIE TOOK HIS KEYS OUT OF HIS POCKET, HELPED RHEA UP FROM HER SEAT, AND LED HER TO HIS CAR. AS JOHNNIE OPENED THE DOOR AND HELPED RHEA INSIDE IN RICO FOLLOWED THEM OUTSIDE AND TOLD RHEA TO STOP. HE TOLD HER SHE NEEDED TO GET INTO HIS VEHICLE INSTEAD BECAUSE THEY NEEDED TO TALK. JOHNNIE ASKED HER IF THAT'S WHAT SHE WANTED TO DO BUT SHE SHOOK HER HEAD IN A NEGATIVE DIRECTION.

AT THAT POINT, JOHNNIE TOLD RICO HE NEEDED TO GO AHEAD AND LET THE LADY CALM DOWN. RICO FEELING ANGRIER BY THE MINUTE, TOLD JOHNNIE HE NEEDED TO MIND HIS OWN DAMN BUSINESS. JOHNNIE

RESPONDED BACK WITH THE SAME AGITATION THAT RICO FELT TELLING HIM SHE WAS HIS BUSINESS, AND HE WOULD BE HANDLING THIS SITUATION RIGHT NOW.

RICO SAW THAT THIS WASN'T GETTING HIM VERY FAR BECAUSE RHEA WOULDN'T COOPERATE WITH ANYTHING HE ASKED, AND HE COULD SEE THAT SHE WAS HYSTERICAL AND NEEDED SOME TIME TO GATHER HER EMOTIONS. RELUCTANTLY, RICO TOLD JOHNNIE THIS ISN'T OVER WHICH HAD JOHNNIE AGREEING WITH HIM BUT SAYING THAT IT WAS OVER FOR NOW. SEEING THAT RICO WAS FINALLY LEAVING HAD RHEA RELAXING A BIT. JOHNNIE TURNED ON THE MUSIC FOR HER AND LEANED THE SEAT BACK. HE THEN TOLD HER TO GIVE HIM A FEW MINUTES AND HE'D BE OUT TO TAKE HER TO HIS PLACE BECAUSE SHE WASN'T IN ANY SHAPE TO BE ALONE TONIGHT.

TRUE TO HIS WORD, HE CAME OUT AND TOOK HER TO HIS HOME AND MADE

HER COMFORTABLE. HIS HOME WAS FAMILIAR TO HER, AND SHE HAD BEEN THERE MANY TIMES BEFORE BUT THAT WAS SEVERAL YEARS AGO WHEN THEY WERE A COUPLE AND ENGAGED. AFTER SETTLING IN WITH A HOT BATH AND CUP OF TEA RHEA BEGAN EXPLAINING THE EVENTS THAT LED HER TO FOLLOW RICO TODAY AND FIND ANSWERS TO HIS BIZARRE BEHAVIOR. JOHNNIE LISTENED PATIENTLY ALLOWING RHEA TO FILL HIM IN ON THE DETAILS TO FORM A MORE ACCURATE PICTURE OF THE SITUATION.

AFTER THE LONG UPSETTING DAY, RHEA FELT EXHAUSTED, SO SHE FELL ASLEEP LYING ACROSS JOHNNIE'S BED. JOHNNIE COVERED HER WITH A WARM BLANKET THEN MADE HIMSELF COMFORTABLE ON HIS LARGE LEATHER SOFA FOR THE NIGHT. WHEN RHEA AWOKE IN THE MORNING AND GOT HER WITS ABOUT HER, SHE THANKED JOHNNIE FOR HIS KINDNESS AND FOR HIS CARE AS HE DROVE HER BACK TO TRIPSY'S LOUNGE TO RETRIEVE HER CAR.

CHAPTER 32

PROPHETIC WORDS

Rhea spent a few days at a hotel alone just to gather her thoughts and to plan her next moves. She knew instinctively that things could never be the same between her and Rico after what she had witnessed. So, there needed to be some grand change in her life, and she needed to be assured that she was on her correct life path and not heading in the wrong direction.

On the third day, she got down on her knees and went before the throne of God and

PRAYED NON-STOP ASKING GOD FOR HIS GUIDANCE, DIRECTION, AND PROTECTION FROM THE EVIL THAT WAS BEING SENT TOWARDS HER VIA SPELL WORK AND VOODOO. SHE PRAYED FOR DIVINE CLARITY AND TO BE COVERED UNDER THE BLOOD COVENANT SO THAT ALL NEGATIVE ATTACKS WOULD BE SENT RIGHT BACK TO THE SENDER WITH INSTANT KARMA ATTACHED.

ONCE RHEA BEGAN TO FEEL THE PEACE THAT ONLY GOD COULD PROVIDE, SHE RETURNED TO THE TABLE PROVIDED BY THE HOTEL ROOM AND MADE HER PLANS. AFTER DRESSING FOR THE DAY AND EATING A LIGHT BREAKFAST OF HOT TEA AND A THOMAS ENGLISH MUFFIN, SHE HEADED IN THE DIRECTION OF HER OLDEST LIVING RELATIVE WHO WAS A WELL-KNOWN PROPHETESS AND GOD GIVEN BIBLICAL ORACLE.

HER AUNTY WAS NOW IN HER MID-EIGHTIES, BUT HER MIND WAS AS SHARP AS A WOMAN IN HER EARLY

TWENTIES. SHE GREETED RHEA WITH A HUG AND KISS AND TOLD HER SHE HAD BEEN EXPECTING HER BECAUSE SHE HAD ALWAYS BEEN VERY TUNED IN TO HER NIECE THROUGH THEIR INTUITIVE GIFTS AND THEIR PROPHETIC BLOODLINE. HER AUNT, SEEING SHE NEEDED REST AND HEALING, SUGGESTED SHE HAVE A GLASS OF WINE AND A RELAXING JACUZZI TUB SOAK WITH SOOTHING SMOOTH JAZZ TO RELAX BEFORE THEY HAD A NICE CHAT.

THE TWO WOMEN TALKED FOR WHAT SEEMED LIKE MANY HOURS BUT IN REALITY, ONLY A FEW HOURS HAD PASSED. WHAT WAS DISCUSSED THAT EVENING, GAVE RHEA A NEW INSIGHT INTO HER TOXIC SITUATION. HOWEVER, AFTER TALKING WITH HER AUNT, SHE FOUND THAT THERE WERE OTHER THINGS TO CONSIDER ABOUT HER SITUATION THAT SHE HADN'T THOUGHT OF BEFORE. AS IN THE PAST, RHEA'S AUNT SHARED PEARLS OF WISDOM AND REMINDED HER OF THE GIFTS SHE'D BEEN GIVEN

THAT WERE PASSED DOWN FROM HER ANCESTORS, INCLUDING HERSELF.

AUNTY TOOK BOTH OF HER NIECE'S HANDS IN HERS AND LOOKED DIRECTLY IN HER EYES, EYES THAT LOOKED SO MUCH LIKE HER OWN, AND SAID THESE WORDS, "IF YOU GIVE DOUBT AND FEAR ANY POWER, THEY ARE SO HUNGRY THEY'LL EAT YOU ALIVE." SHE CONTINUED BY SAYING HOW PROUD SHE AND HER ANCESTORS WERE OF THE WOMAN SHE'D BECOME AFTER EDUCATING HERSELF AND FOLLOWING THE PATH THAT GOD HAD ORDAINED FOR HER AND CORRECTING THE MISTAKES OF HER PAST.

SHE TOLD RHEA THAT NO MATTER HOW THINGS SEEM RIGHT NOW, SHE SHOULD NOT CLOSE HERSELF OFF TO ANYTHING BECAUSE GOD WAS IN CONTROL OF THIS SITUATION, AND IT WAS TRULY DIVINELY GUIDED. SHE CONTINUED BY TELLING HER NIECE THAT VERY SOON, ALL WOULD BE REVEALED TO HER, AND SHE WOULD

UNDERSTAND THAT SOME THINGS ARE JUST ILLUSIONS. SHE TOLD RHEA THAT GOD AND THE ANCESTORS HAD TO STEP IN BECAUSE DARK FORCES WERE AT PLAY HERE. RHEA LISTENED INTENTLY TO HER AUNTY AND FELT THAT HER AUNT KNEW MUCH MORE THAN WHAT SHE WAS SHARING BUT SHE CERTAINLY APPRECIATED EVERY WORD.

RHEA'S AUNT THEN TOLD HER THAT EVERY VISION SHE HAS AND EVERY STEP SHE MAKES SHOULD BE ALIGNED WITH HER LIFE PATH WHICH WILL LEAD HER TO HER NORTH STAR. RHEA TOLD HER AUNT THAT SHE WOULD BE STAYING AT THE RANCH WITH HER FOR A FEW DAYS ALLOWING HERSELF TO RELAX, REFLECT AND GATHER HER THOUGHTS. HER AUNT WAS DELIGHTED TO HAVE HER VISIT, AS ALWAYS. TO RHEA, HER AUNT'S RANCH WAS MORE LIKE HOME THAN ANY PLACE OTHER THAN HER OWN. IT WAS HER SAFE PLACE TO LAND.

CHAPTER 33

A DIVINE MESSENGER

That night, Rhea decided to study some of the materials she'd brought with her to keep herself occupied and to broaden her knowledge about the Twin Flame Connection. What she discovered had her head reeling and wondering why God would allow so many complications connected with this Divine pair before they finally surrendered their egos to come into union? It was so overwhelming she tossed the material aside and picked up her Bible instead.

FEELING BOTH MENTALLY AND PHYSICALLY EXHAUSTED AND A BIT OVERWHELMED, RHEA DRIFTED OFF TO SLEEP WITH THE BIBLE ON HER CHEST WHILE LISTENING TO OPRAH AND OTHER MOTIVATIONAL SPEAKERS ON VIDEO SHE'D RECORDED TO LISTEN TO AT BEDTIME FOR RELAXATION. SHE WAS ACCUSTOMED TO HAVING A SERIES OF DREAMS, VISIONS, AND DOWNLOADS DURING SLEEP BECAUSE SHE KNEW THIS WAS WHERE SHE RECEIVED HER MESSAGES FROM GOD.

EVEN AS A LITTLE GIRL, AND BEFORE SHE KNEW WHAT HER GIFTS WERE, SHE HAD VIVID DREAMS AND VISIONS DURING THE NIGHT WHILE SHE SLEPT. SHE TRIED TO REMEMBER WHAT HAPPENED IN THEM BUT SOMETIMES THEY WERE HARD TO REMEMBER. HOWEVER, WHEN GOD WANTED TO GIVE HER A MESSAGE, SHE HEARD IT LOUD AND CLEAR. THIS NIGHT WAS CERTAINLY ONE FILLED WITH A DIVINE ORDER THAT SHE KNEW SHE MUST HEED.

IN THE DREAM RHEA COULD SEE BEAUTIFUL TREES, FLOWERS, AND MAGNIFICENT BIRDS OF EVERY COLOR CHIRPING. SHE COULD HEAR THE SOUND OF SOFT HARP MUSIC PLAYING IN THE DISTANCE. SHE LOOKED UPWARD KNOWING THAT THE BIRDS WERE GOD'S MESSENGERS, AND THEY MUST BE HERE WITH SOMETHING TO SHARE. IN THE DISTANCE SHE COULD HERE VOICES SPEAKING BUT COULDN'T QUITE MAKE OUT WHAT WAS BEING SPOKEN. SUDDENLY A VOICE GENTLY CALLED HER BY NAME, A VOICE SHE WAS SURPRISED TO RECOGNIZE AS OPRAH WINFREY'S!

OPRAH BEGAN BY SAYING HELLO, I WAS SENT BY THE DIVINE, AND THAT GOD HAD CHOSEN HER TO BE THE MESSENGER TODAY. SHE TOLD RHEA TO RELAX ON A NEARBY BENCH AND LISTEN. RHEA SAT IMMEDIATELY TOO MESMERIZED BY THE BEAUTIFUL AND TALENTED LADY TO EVEN SPEAK. WHAT OPRAH SPOKE TO HER THAT NIGHT WAS STRAIGHT FROM GOD HIMSELF AND RHEA KNEW INTUITIVELY

THAT THE WORDS WERE SPOKEN AS REASSURANCE THAT SHE WAS NOT ALONE ON THIS DIFFICULT JOURNEY.

OPRAH TOLD HER THAT SHE DIDN'T HAVE TO FEAR THAT GOD'S PROTECTION WAS SURROUNDING HER AND THAT NO WEAPON FORMED AGAINST HER WOULD PROSPER. SHE TOLD RHEA THAT, THAT INCLUDED SPELL WORK, AND THAT THOSE PRACTICING WITH THE DARK ARTS WERE ALREADY BEING SEVERELY DEALT WITH. SHE ALSO SAID THAT GOD HAS SAID THAT HER DIVINE COUNTERPART HAS COMMITTED OR BROKEN SEVERAL SPIRITUAL LAWS AGAINST HER AND THAT BECAUSE HE HAS REFUSED TO OBEY HIS SPIRITUAL CONTRACT TO BE ON THE LIFE PATH THAT HE SIGNED UP FOR ORIGINALLY, HE WOULD BE DEALT SEVERE KARMA.

SHE SAID THAT GOD MAY SEVER OR CUT THE SOUL CORD TO DESTROY THE CONTRACT AND THE UNION BETWEEN THE TWINS IF HE DOESN'T DO HIS SHADOW WORK AND HEAL FROM HIS

CHILDHOOD WOUNDS WHICH HAS HIM LIVING IN DEVIL MENTALITY. SHE SAID THAT BECAUSE THEY WERE INDEED TWIN FLAMES WHO SHARED A SOUL, THE GIFTS THAT WERE GIVEN TO RHEA WERE ALSO GIVEN HIM, BUT THAT HE WAS USING HIS NEGATIVELY FOR DARK SPELL WORK WHICH GOES AGAINST GOD AND HER.

SHE CONTINUED BY SAYING THAT AS A RESULT, RICO'S GIFTS WOULD BE STRIPPED FROM HIM AND GIVEN TO HER AS SOON AS THE SOUL CORD WAS CUT, AND THAT GOD HIMSELF WOULD SEND HER A SOULMATE WHO WOULD LOVE AND HONOR HER AND TREAT HER WITH RESPECT UNTIL THE END OF THEIR TIME HERE ON EARTH. SHE REMINDED RHEA THAT THERE IS ONLY ONE TWIN FLAME BUT SEVERAL SOULMATES AND THAT TWINS WERE VERY RARE WHICH IS WHY THE DIVINE STEPPED IN AND IS NOT PLEASED WITH HER COUNTERPART.

SHE CONTINUED BY TELLING RHEA THAT SHE WAS INDEED ON HER

RIGHT PATH AND THAT SHE NEEDED TO SURRENDER ALL TO THE DIVINE AND TRUST THAT ALL WOULD BE REVEALED SOON. SHE ALSO TOLD HER TO CONTINUE TO POUR INTO HER OWN CUPS AND KEEP THEM FULL. SHE REMINDED HER TO NEVER RELINQUISH HER POWER BY PRETENDING HER GIFTS DIDN'T EXIST, BECAUSE HER LIGHT SHINES SO BRIGHT IT EXPOSES THE DEMONS IN PEOPLE AND THAT IS WHAT INTIMIDATES THEM.

SHE TOLD RHEA TO TAKE HER WOUNDS AND TURN THEM INTO WISDOM, AND HER WISDOM INTO GOLD BECAUSE HER GIFTS WERE GIVEN TO HER FOR A REASON AND THAT GOD IS ONLY SHARPENING HER SKILLS, STRENGTHENING HER GIFTS AND ILLUMINATING ONES THAT SHE HADN'T REALIZED WERE THERE. SHE FINISHED BY SAYING SHE MUST ALIGN HERSELF WITH HER PURPOSE, AND THAT SHE MUST LEARN TO USE HER GIFTS AND TALENTS IN SERVICE TO THE WORLD SO THAT IT NO LONGER

BECOMES A JOB IT BECOMES AN OFFERING TO THE WORLD.

HEARING THOSE WORDS BROUGHT TEARS TO RHEA'S EYES AND SHE AWAKENED CRYING SOFTLY BUT KNOWING NOW WHAT HER PURPOSE WAS IN THIS LIFE. SHE VOWED TO NEVER AGAIN ALLOW ANYONE TO DEFLECT HER FROM HER PATH NO MATTER HOW SHE FELT FOR THEM.

CHAPTER 34

ENLIGHTENMENT

WHEN RHEA FINALLY STOPPED CRYING, SHE REALIZED THAT THE TEARS SHE SHED WERE NO LONGER DUE TO SADNESS BUT QUITE THE OPPOSITE. THEY WERE IN FACT, TEARS OF GRATITUDE. SHE WAS SO GRATEFUL THAT THE ALMIGHTY HAD INDEED HEARD HER PRAYERS AND SENT SOMEONE SHE BOTH LOVED AND RESPECTED TO GIVE HER REASSURANCE AND GUIDANCE REGARDING HER LIFE PATH. RHEA REALIZED THAT SHE HAD FALLEN ASLEEP IN THE PAST, LISTENING TO A MOTIVATIONAL SPEECH BY OPRAH WINFREY AND SOME OF THE WORDS SHE'D HEARD IN HER DREAM WERE

FROM ONE OF THE SPEECHES OPRAH HAD GIVEN WHICH SHE'D LISTENED TO BEFORE.

SECRETLY, SHE HAD ALWAYS ADMIRED OPRAH AND SAID ONCE OR TWICE THAT OPRAH DIDN'T KNOW THIS YET, BUT SHE AND GAYLE'S FRIENDSHIP WAS IN REALITY SUPPOSED TO BE A TRIANGLE FOR THREE AND NOT A LINE FOR TWO BECAUSE SHE WAS MOST CERTAINLY THE THIRD PERSON IN THE FRIENDSHIP THAT THEY WERE YET TO MEET. SHE LAUGHED ALOUD AT THAT THEORY STILL HOPING SOMEDAY IT WOULD BECOME A REALITY.

THE NEXT DAY, RHEA SAID GOODBYE TO HER AUNTY FEELING REFRESHED, ENLIGHTENED, AND READY TO FACE WHATEVER DEMONS WERE HEADED HER WAY. KNOWING GOD HAD SENT HIS ARCH ANGELS, SPIRIT GUIDES, AND HER BELOVED ANCESTORS TO WATCH OVER AND PROTECT HER, HAD HER BREATHING A SIGH OF RELIEF.

RHEA REFLECTED ON EVERYTHING THAT HAD HER FEELING AS IF HER LIFE WAS FINALLY COMING BACK INTO BALANCE. SHE ACCEPTED THE FACT THAT RICO HAD SIMPLY MISHANDLED HER AND THEIR RELATIONSHIP IN THIS CONNECTION. SHE WAS UPSET ABOUT IT, BUT SHE DID TAKE A SMALL PART OF THE BLAME BECAUSE SHE ALLOWED THIS TOXIC BEHAVIOR AND REFUSED TO SEE THE RED FLAGS THAT WERE FLYING FULL MASS. SHE DREW IN A DEEP SIGH OF REGRET AND DECIDED IT WAS TIME TO FORGIVE HERSELF AND MOVE ON WITH THE VALUABLE LESSONS THIS SITUATION HAD SO PAINFULLY TAUGHT HER.

IN HER FAMILIAR SURROUNDINGS, RHEA MADE PLANS TO MOVE FORWARD WITH A FEW PROJECTS THAT WERE ALREADY IN PROGRESS BUT HAD BEEN PLACED ON THE BACK BURNER. AS SOON AS DINNER WAS EATEN, SHE TOOK A NICE RELAXING SPIRITUAL CLEANSING BATH TRYING TO RID HERSELF OF ANY RESIDUAL TOXIC ENERGY THAT MIGHT HAVE BEEN

LEFT BEHIND FROM HER PREVIOUS RELATIONSHIP.

SHE BURNED CANDLES, INCENSE, AND SAGE TO PURIFY HER SPACE. SHE DECIDED THAT SHE WOULD MAINTAIN HER CELIBACY AND THE NEXT RELATIONSHIP IF THERE EVER WAS A NEXT, SHE WOULD TAKE AS LONG AS SHE NEEDED TO FEEL ABLE TO TRUST HIM WITH ANYTHING RELATED TO HER AND ESPECIALLY WHEN IT CAME TO INTIMACY.

JUST AS SHE WAS ABOUT TO CALL IT A NIGHT, HER CELL PHONE RANG. "HELLO IS THIS RHEA RICHARDS?" SHE REPLIED YES TO THE MALE VOICE THAT SOUNDED DEEP AND BARITONE. "WHOSE SPEAKING, AND HOW MIGHT I HELP YOU?" THE DEEP VOICE CONTINUED BY SAYING HE DIDN'T KNOW IF RICO ROBINS EVER MENTIONED HIM TO HER BEFORE, BUT HE WAS HIS VERY CLOSEST FRIEND, AND HE NEEDED TO SEE HER TO TELL HER SOME VERY IMPORTANT INFORMATION THAT WOULD CERTAINLY

BE SOMETHING SHE'D APPRECIATE KNOWING. RHEA COULDN'T DENY THAT SHE WAS INTRIGUED AND CURIOUS. SO, SHE AGREED TO MEET WITH HIM THE NEXT DAY AT A PARK IN THE BROADLAND SHOPPING AREA DURING LUNCHTIME TO TALK.

RHEA HAD TO ADMIT SHE WAS A LITTLE NERVOUS AND ANXIOUS WONDERING WHAT THIS INFORMATION COULD BE. SHE ARRIVED A LITTLE EARLY TO THE MEETING SPOT TO SURVEY THE SURROUNDINGS AND TO MAKE SURE THIS WASN'T SOME TYPE OF SET-UP OR ANYTHING THAT WOULD MAKE HER INTUITION GO INTO HIGH GEAR. AFTER FEELING A SENSE OF CALMNESS, SHE WAITED UNTIL HIS ARRIVAL AND FELT RELAXED IN HIS PRESCENCE. HE ASKED HER IF SHE HAD TIME TO HAVE A SERIOUS CONVERSATION, OR WAS THERE SOMEWHERE ELSE SHE NEEDED TO BE? SHE ASSURED HIM THAT HER SCHEDULE WAS CLEAR AND THAT HE SHOULD SPEAK FREELY.

HE BEGAN BY TELLING HER THAT HE WAS THE ONE WHO WAS WITH RICO AT THE COMMUNITY BLOCK PARTY WHEN HE INSISTED, SHE SLIP HIM HER NUMBER. SHE RECALLED HIM STANDING WITH SOMEONE, BUT SHE COULD NOT HAVE REMEMBERED WHO THAT PERSON WAS. HE TOLD HER THAT HE KNEW WHEN THE RELATIONSHIP HAD JUMPED-OFF AND HE WAS WELL AWARE OF THE ROLLER-COASTER RIDE IT HAD BEEN ON EVER SINCE.

HE KNEW INTIMATE DETAILS ABOUT THE TIMES SHE BROKE IT OFF WITH HIM AND TOLD HIM SHE WAS NOT A SIDE CHICK OR ONE OF HIS OPTIONS. HE COUNTED SIX TIMES IN ALL OVER THE LAST TWO YEARS BUT MENTIONED THAT THE LAST TIME WAS DIFFERENT BECAUSE IT WAS THE FIRST TIME, SHE'D EVER SAID SHE WAS MOVING ON. HE TOLD HER THAT RICO WAS DEFINITELY AFFECTED BY THOSE WORDS. HE THEN ASKED IF SHE IN FACT REALLY MOVED ON?

RHEA SHOOK HER HEAD NO, THAT SHE WASN'T EVEN ENTERTAINING THE THOUGHT OF A NEW RELATIONSHIP AND AT THE MOMENT, SHE WAS ONLY INTERESTED IN HER OWN SPIRITUAL GROWTH AND ENLIGHTENMENT. HE THEN BEGAN TO EXPLAIN HIS REASON FOR CALLING. HE STARTED BY TELLING RHEA THAT HE WAS WELL AWARE OF THE WAY RICO HAD TREATED HER IN THIS RELATIONSHIP AND HE WAS TRULY EMBARRASSED AND BEYOND SORRY FOR THE WAY HE BEHAVED. BUT RHEA SHOOK HER HEAD AND SAID THAT THAT WASN'T THE CASE BECAUSE IF A PERSON WERE GENUINELY SORRY, THEY WOULD HAVE OWNED UP TO THEIR MISTAKES, STOPPED THE LIES AND APOLOGIZED FOR BRINGING DISHONOR TO HER NAME IN THE COMMUNITY AND TO DATE, HE HAS DONE NONE OF THAT.

HE THEN TOLD RHEA THAT AROUND THE TIME RICO STARTED ACTING LIKE AN ASSHOLE, HE HAD MET SOMEONE WHO HAD CAUGHT HIS EYE DURING

ONE OF THE TIMES WHEN SHE WALKED AWAY. HE WAS SO MAD AND HURT, HE WENT DRINKING AND ENDED UP AT ONE OF THE STRIP CLUBS.

THAT NIGHT, HE MET SOMEONE WHO HE THOUGHT WAS HIS PERFECT MATCH AND FELL FOR HER RIGHT AWAY. ME AND THE BOYS TRIED TO TALK TO HIM AND TELL HIM TO SLOW DOWN BECAUSE HE WAS MOVING ENTIRELY TOO FAST WITH THIS PERSON, BUT HIS ANSWER WAS THAT HE NEEDED TO REPLACE YOU BY GIVING HIS HEART TO SOMEONE WHO WOULD APPRECIATE IT AND STOP LEAVING HIM. WHAT WAS MEANT TO BE A ONE NIGHT STAND ONLY, TURNED INTO A NIGHTMARE RELATIONSHIP. SHE PUT ON A FALSE MASK AND ACTED ALL SHY AND MADE HIM WAIT TWO MONTHS TO BECOME INTIMATE WITH HER WHICH IMPRESSED HIM. SHE WAS ALL FAKE AS HELL AND THE BIGGEST ESCORT IN THE BUSINESS.

AFTER THE INTIMACY BEGAN, SHE TOLD HIM SHE WAS PREGNANT,

AND HE HAD TO MARRY HER. BUT BY THEN, MISSING YOU, HE HAD COME BACK TO YOU AS HE USUALLY DID AND RECONCILED YOU GUY'S RELATIONSHIP WITHOUT TELLING YOU WHAT WAS UP OR BREAKING THINGS OFF WITH HER FIRST. IN FACT, HE DID THE OPPOSITE AND TOLD YOU TO FIND A SPOT, MAKING YOU THINK IT WAS FOR HIM, BUT IT WAS FOR HIM AND HER. WE ALL LOOKED AT HIM DIFFERENTLY AFTER THAT NOT KNOWING WHO IN THE HELL THIS DOG ASS DUDE WAS. NO ONE COULD BELIEVE HE WAS DOING YOU LIKE THIS WHEN ALL YOU'D EVER SHOWN HIM WAS KINDNESS AND LOVE.

WE ALL TRIED TALKING TO HIM, BUT HE WASN'T HIMSELF AND ME AND THE REST OF HIS BOYS KNEW SOMETHING WAS SERIOUSLY WRONG, SO WE DECIDED TO INVESTIGATE FOR OURSELVES. ONE WEEKEND AFTER WE HUNG OUT AND HE GOT HIS USUAL PARTY ON, HE BEGAN TALKING ABOUT YOU NEGATIVELY AND CRITICIZING YOU BY TELLING US ABOUT THE

PRIVATE INTIMATE DETAILS OF YOUR CONNECTION. HE WAS OUT OF LINE, AND WE ALL TOLD HIM TO STOP.

HE WAS FEELING HIMSELF AND DECIDED TO CALL YOU TO MAKE YOU SAY SOMETHING THAT MADE HIM UPSET SO HE COULD YELL AT YOU, DISRESPECT YOU, AND SLAM THE PHONE DOWN IN FRONT OF US. HE THOUGHT DOING THIS WAS MAKING HIM LOOK LIKE HE WAS ALL THAT. WE ALL LOST A LOT OF RESPECT FOR HIM BEHIND THAT BECAUSE THIS WAS SOMEONE WE DIDN'T KNOW. HE JUST KEPT SAYING THAT NO MATTER WHAT HE DID TO YOU, YOU WOULD TOLERATE IT AS LONG AS HE WAS BRINGING YOU WHAT YOU CRAVED. I WILL ADMIT THAT ONE OR TWO OF US FOUND IT FUNNY AND LAUGHED. BUT FOR ME, IT WASN'T FUNNY, AND I KNOW HOW KARMA WORKS ESPECIALLY FOR SOMEONE WHO DIDN'T DO ANYTHING TO DESERVE THIS KIND OF TREATMENT.

RHEA ADMITTED THAT SHE'D HAD A FALLING OUT WITH HER SISTER AROUND THAT TIME ABOUT RUMORS THAT HAD GOTTEN BACK TO HER ABOUT SOME THINGS HE HAD SUPPOSEDLY SAID, AND HOW SHE DEFENDED THE RELATIONSHIP. FOR THE FIRST TIME IN HER LIFE, SHE AND HER SISTER HAD STOPPED SPEAKING. LATER HER SISTER CALLED CRYING AND APOLOGIZING SAYING SHE JUST DIDN'T WANT HER TO GET HURT. LATER, RHEA APOLOGIZED TO HER SISTER AND TOLD HER SHE WAS RIGHT AFTER INVESTIGATING THE RUMORS FOR HERSELF.

RICO'S FRIEND CONTINUED TELLING RHEA THAT HE FOLLOWED RICO HOME THAT NIGHT TO MAKE SURE HIS FRIEND GOT THERE SAFELY. HE SAID THAT WHAT HE DISCOVERED THAT NIGHT HAD HIM MORE CONCERNED THAN ANYTHING ELSE. HE SAID HE FOLLOWED FOR A LITTLE WHILE AT A NICE DISTANCE BUT SOON HE LOST HIM. AT THAT POINT, HE SAID HE WENT DIRECTLY TO THE HOUSE ON

HIS OWN BUT ONCE HE GOT THERE RICO WAS NO WHERE TO BE SEEN SO I PEERED IN THE BACK WINDOW TO SEE IF ANYONE WAS UP. BUT WHAT I SAW STILL GIVES ME NIGHTMARES.

SHE WAS IN THE KITCHEN DOING GROSS THINGS AND PUTTING THINGS IN HIS FOOD AND DRINKS. SHE THEN STARTED CHANTING AND DOING BLOOD RITUALS AND I COULDN'T WATCH ANYMORE. RHEA COULD ONLY IMAGINE WHAT HE SAW AND REMEMBERED TELLING RICO TO STOP EATING EVERYONE'S FOOD BECAUSE HE HAD BEEN SUFFERING WITH GASTROINTESTINAL PROBLEMS A LOT. NOW THIS WAS CERTAINLY CONFIRMATION OF WHAT HER INTUITION HAD PICKED UP ON A WHILE BACK.

CHAPTER 35

RUMORS CLARIFIED

Rico's friend then asked Rhea if she felt okay with sharing the rumors she'd heard with him so he could clarify which ones were true or just plain lies. She apologized for some of the intimate details that would be attached to the rumors she'd heard, it was necessary for him to get the complete picture. She started by explaining that she and Rico had a thing for outside, intimate moments and especially in the back of his jeep.

She told him that as a married woman who had been treated

WITH ADORATION AND PAMPERED THROUGHOUT THE YEARS, SHE HAD SPENT LOTS OF TIME IN FIVE-STAR RESORTS AND SOME OF THE BEST HOTELS ON THE WEST COAST AND BEYOND. SHE ADMITTED SHE HAD LOVED THE CHILD-LIKE CAREFREE NATURE OF THEIR RELATIONSHIP AND CONSIDERED IT AN ADVENTUROUS THING BETWEEN THEM. SHE SAID THAT FOR HER, IT REMINDED HER OF THE DAYS WHEN THEY GREW UP HAVING THESE TYPES OF AFFAIRS AT THE DRIVE-IN OR WHEREVER THEY CONSIDERED SOMEWHERE TABU.

BUT THE RUMORS SHE HEARD THAT HE'D SPREAD MADE HER SEEM AS IF SHE WERE TREATED LIKE A TWO-DOLLAR WHORE WHO HAD SEX IN THE BACK SEAT OF HIS CAR BUT WAS NEVER GIVEN THE RESPECT OR LUXURY OF SPENDING A DIME ON HER IN A HOTEL OR A FIVE-STAR RESORT WHICH SHE WAS ACCUSTOMED TO.

HIS WORDS MADE IT SEEM AS IF SHE WEREN'T WORTHY OF BEING

TREATED AS THE DIVINE FEMININE THAT GOD HAD SENT TO HIM, BUT INSTEAD, AS SOME DIRTY LITTLE SECRET TO BE HIDDEN AWAY FOR HIS SEXUAL PLEASURES. SHE SAID THAT IN REALITY, THE DIVINE HIMSELF ACTUALLY HID HER WORTH AND VALUE FROM HIM TO PROVE IF HE WAS HER TRUE DIVINE MASCULINE. BUT HE CHOSE SOMEONE WHO MIRRORED HIS TOXICITY AND INSTEAD TREATED THE WRONG PERSON AS HIS DIVINE COUNTERPART WHICH ANGERED GOD AND BROUGHT KARMA DOWN ON HIM AND HIS NASTY STD HAVING WHORE.

SHE CONTINUED BY TELLING HIM SHE'D HEARD HE SAID BECAUSE SHE WAS MARRIED BEFORE, SHE WASN'T GOING TO MAKE HIM ONE OF HER EX-HUSBANDS, AND THAT HE CHOSE A PERSON WHO WAS OPPOSITE FROM HER TO TALK ABOUT HER BEHIND HER BACK NEVER REALIZING HE WAS THE ONE BEING PLAYED BY THIS LOW VIBRATING FEMALE.

SHE TOLD HIM THAT SHE'D HEARD HE'D LIED AND SAID SHE WAS EITHER BI-POLAR OR EMOTIONALLY IMBALANCED AND HAD SCHIZOPHRENIA WHEN IN FACT, THAT WAS REALLY WHAT THE PERSON HE HAD CHOSEN OVER HER MENTAL CONDITIONS WERE WHICH EVERYONE KNEW ABOUT BUT HIM UNTIL IT WAS TOO LATE.

RHEA CONTINUED SAYING EVERY TIME SHE TRIED TO HAVE AN ADULT CONVERSATION WITH RICO TO ADDRESS THE RUMORS AND ISSUES IN THEIR CONNECTION HE'D REFUSE AND START AN ARGUMENT BY CALLING HER A DRAMA QUEEN WHO LIKED TO KEEP UP DRAMA. SHE'D ALSO HEARD THAT HE LIED AND TOLD PEOPLE THAT SHE WAS SELFISH WITH HER MONEY AND ENERGY AND A GOLD DIGGER WHO ONLY WANTED HIM FOR WHAT HE COULD PROVIDE HER.

RHEA EXPLAINED THAT SHE ALSO CONTINUED TRYING SEVERAL TIMES ASKING HIM ABOUT THE RUMORS, BUT HE WOULD NEVER HAVE

CONVERSATIONS WITH HER ABOUT ANYTHING BECAUSE HE DIDN'T WANT HIS SECRETS EXPOSED. AFTER HEARING THE LATEST RUMORS RHEA ADMITTED THAT ONE DAY IT HAD ALL BECOME TOO MUCH, AND SHE WOULD NOT ALLOW RICO TO DISMISS HER CONCERNS ANY LONGER. SHE SAID SHE TOLD HIM IF HE WASN'T GOING TO RESPOND TO HER QUESTIONS THEN HE WAS DAMN WELL GOING TO HEAR HER OUT OR HE COULD KEEP IT MOVING.

SHE FELT IT WAS TIME HE DECIDED WHICH DIRECTION HE WANTED THEIR RELATIONSHIP TO GO IN BECAUSE SHE WASN'T GOING TO BE ANYONE'S SIDEPIECE. AFTER TELLING HIM ALL THE NEGATIVE TALK THAT HAD MADE IT BACK TO HER FROM THE STREETS, SHE LOOKED DIRECTLY INTO HIS EYES AND TOLD HIM SHE DIDN'T KNOW WHO HE WAS INVOLVED WITH BUT WHOMEVER SHE WAS IT WAS TIME TO SEND HER ASS PACKING.

SHE ALSO TOLD HIM THAT HE NEEDED TO MAN UP AND EITHER TAKE HIS BALLS OUT OF HER POCKETBOOK AND ATTACH THEM BACK ON OR TAKE HIS ASS TO THE WIZARD OF OZ AS THE COWARDLY LION AND GET HIMSELF SOME DAMN COURAGE TO STAND UP TO HIS THIS WOMAN. SHE SAID THAT'S WHEN SHE DECIDED TO PUT THEIR RELATIONSHIP ON PERMANENT PAUSE.

HE ASKED QUIETLY WAS THERE ANYTHING ELSE SHE'D HEARD? SHE SAID YES, THE ONE THAT CUT THE DEEPEST WAS THAT SHE WAS A LIAR WHO HAD CHEATED ON HIM AND WAS NEVER FAITHFUL THROUGHOUT THE ENTIRE RELATIONSHIP WHICH IS WHY SHE HAD WALKED AWAY FROM HIM ON NUMEROUS OCCASIONS JUST TO BE WITH OTHER GUYS.

BY NOW RHEA WAS CRYING AND WITH TEARS STREAMING DOWN HER FACE SHE CONTINUED TO EXPLAIN THE RUMORS SHE'D HEARD ABOUT RICO BUT NOT BEFORE HE ASKED IF SHE WANTED TO STOP. SHE SHOOK

HER HEAD NO AND CONTINUED AFTER DRYING HER TEARS WITH A KLEENEX FROM HER PURSE. SHE TOLD HIM THAT SHE'D HEARD ABOUT HIS AFFAIR WITH A YOUNG PROSTITUTE WHO HE SUPPOSEDLY IMPREGNATED, AND THAT HE HAD MARRIED AND MOVED IN WITH HER BECAUSE SHE SUPPOSEDLY HAD MORE CHILDREN THAT WERE HIS.

SHE SAID SHE'D HEARD HE LIKED TO INVOLVE HIMSELF WITH THREESOMES AND ORGIES AND THAT HE HAD A TRANSGENDER LOVER WHO WAS SECRETLY A MALE WHO HE HAD BEEN IN A LONG- TERM RELATIONSHIP WITH. SHE TOLD HIM RUMOR HAD IT, THAT HE PRACTICED GAY FOR PAY IN THE LBGT COMMUNITY AND THAT SHE'D HEARD HE HAD A SEX ADDICTION, DRUG AND ALCOHOL ADDICTIONS; AND WHAT HE DIDN'T SPEND ON HIS HABITS, WAS SPENT ON CHILD SUPPORT FOR HIDDEN CHILDREN THAT HE HAD SECRETLY FATHERED.

AT THAT POINT, SHE THOUGHT SHE HEARD HIM SNICKER JUST A LITTLE,

BUT SHE CONTINUED ANYHOW. SHE TOLD HIM THAT HE BROUGHT ALL HIS EARNINGS TO THE STRIPPER, OR SEX WORKER WHO WAS SECRETLY INVOLVED WITH SOMEONE IN HIS FAMILY AND THE CHILD SHE WAS EITHER CARRYING OR THAT HAD RECENTLY BEEN BORN, WAS NOT FATHERED BY RICO, BUT SOMEONE CLOSE TO HIM AND HE WAS LIED TO FOR CHILD SUPPORT. AND TO TOP IT OFF, HE'S ALSO BEEN CHEATING ON HER FOR A CO-WORKER WHOM HE HAD A SEXUAL AFFAIR WITH BOTH DURING WORK AND AFTER IN THE EVENINGS. THIS IS ANOTHER WOMAN WHO RUMOR SAYS IS CLAIMING HE ALSO IMPREGNATED HER TOO.

RHEA CONTINUED SAYING, SHE'D HEARD THAT HE HAD FOOLISHLY STARTED A BUSINESS WITH THIS WOMAN INSTEAD OF WITH RHEA, AS SHE'D SUGGESTED THEY DO, AND WAS NOW FEELING REGRETFUL BECAUSE SHE SUPPOSEDLY USED ALL THE FINANCES FROM THE ONLINE BUSINESS ON DRUGS, AND

INSIGNIFICANT THINGS INSTEAD OF THE BUSINESS AND IT WAS FAILING. SHE SAID THAT THE BUZZ AROUND THE COMMUNITY, KNOWS THAT THE KARMIC HE INVESTED ALL HIS TIME, MONEY AND ENERGY ON WAS SECRETLY USING HIS HARD-EARNED MONEY TO BUILD WITH SOMEONE ELSE WHO SHE PLANNED EVENTUALLY TO LEAVE HIM FOR THE SAME WAY HE'D LEFT TO HER.

SHE SAID SHE ALSO HEARD HE WAS BEING INVESTIGATED FOR SWINDLING WOMEN AND OTHERS OUT OF THEIR MONEY THROUGH SEX BOMBING THEM, AND THAT HE WAS SUSPECTED OF BEING THE ONE THEY CALLED "THE TINDER SWINDLER" WHO HAS MULTIPLE SOCIAL MEDIA ACCOUNTS ON ALL SITES TO TARGET INDIVIDUALS FOR THEIR MONEY. THAT'S ABOUT ALL I CAN REMEMBER AT THE MOMENT, RHEA ADMITTED.

RICO'S FRIEND STARTED BY APOLOGIZING FOR THE TRAUMA SHE'D EXPERIENCED THROUGHOUT

THIS WHOLE ORDEAL. WHICH WAS SOMETHING RICO HAD NEVER DONE. HE TOLD HER THAT THE NIGHT HE'D FOLLOWED RICO WASN'T THE ONLY TIME HE'D WITNESSED DARK MAGIC AT PLAY AND THAT HE'D SAW A GROUP OF THE DARK WITCH AND HER COVEN FRIENDS ONE NIGHT DO SOME VILE RITUALISTIC STUFF TO HIM WHILE HE WAS HEAVILY UNDER THE INFLUENCE.

HE SAID HE DIDN'T RECOGNIZE THESE WOMEN, BUT THEY WERE VERY PHYSICAL WITH RICO AND THAT THE RITUALS MOST DEFINITELY INCLUDED SEX MAGIC. HE ADMITTED THAT IT WAS ALL TRULY DISGUSTING AND THAT HE HAD TO TURN AWAY SEVERAL TIMES, BUT HE HAD TO STAY TO MAKE SURE RICO DIDN'T END UP AS SOME DEAD SACRIFICE FOR THE GROUP.

SO, WHAT I AM SAYING IS THAT UNTIL HE WOKE UP AND BECAME AWARE OF WHAT WAS ACTUALLY BEING DONE TO HIM, HE WASN'T THE MAN YOU KNEW AND FELL FOR. NOW HE IS AND YOU WERE THE CAUSE OF HIM WAKING UP

AND GETTING HIS SPIRITUALITY BACK. HE'S TAKING HIS LIFE BACK RHEA, AND HE NEEDS YOU IN IT.

HE ALSO TOLD RHEA THAT RICO HAD BEEN PLAYING ALONG WITH THE KARMIC DARK WITCH AND GOING TO THE RITUALS TO SEE WHAT THE COVEN WAS DOING SO HE COULD TAKE THE INFORMATION TO A HIGH PRIESTESS FRIEND TO UNDO THE SPELL WORK ON HER. HE SAID THAT RICO HAD BEEN ACTING OUT AS HYPER-SEXUAL SLEEPING WITH SEVERAL ONE-NIGHT STANDS BECAUSE THE KARMIC HAD PLACED A SEX-BINDING SPELL ON HIM TO BIND HIM TO HER SEXUALLY, BUT THE SPELL BACKFIRED AND GAVE HIM A SEXUAL ADDICTION INSTEAD AND ESPECIALLY TOWARDS YOU BECAUSE YOU ARE HIS SEXUAL DESIRE.

HE HAS FINALLY RETURNED TO US AND CANNOT BELIEVE THE WAY HE TREATED THE LOVE OF HIS LIFE. HE HAD ALWAYS CALLED YOU HIS STAR AND SAID YOU WERE HIS TOTAL PACKAGE. RHEA INTERRUPTED AND

SAID HOW HE HAD OFTEN REFERRED TO HER AS THE HIS TOTAL PACKAGE BUT THE LAST TIME HE SAID IT, HER RESPONSE WAS, IF SHE WAS THE TOTAL PACKAGE THEN SHE MUST BE AT THE WRONG DAMN ADDRESS.

HIS FRIEND LAUGHED AND TOLD RHEA THAT RICO NEEDED A CHANCE TO HEAL, AND SO DID SHE BECAUSE THEY WERE BOTH VICTIMS OF DARK FORCES THAT RICO HAS BEEN TRYING TO PROTECT HER AND HIMSELF FROM THE DARK MAGIC UNTIL HE CAN LEAVE SAFELY. HE TOLD HER THAT RICO AND EVEN HE HIMSELF HAS FOLLOWED HER ON NUMEROUS OCCASIONS WHEN THREATS WERE BEING MADE AGAINST HER.

HE SAID THAT THE WITCH KNEW ALL ABOUT HER FROM THE TEXT MESSAGES AND PICTURES SHE'D FOUND IN HIS PHONE AND THAT HE'D LIED AND TOLD EVERYONE THAT HE NO LONGER HAS ANYTHING TO DO WITH YOU AND TO BE MORE CONVINCING, HE MADE IT SOUND AS IF YOU REPULSED HIM AND

HE HATED YOU AND WAS ON BOARD WITH WHATEVER EVIL PLANS THEY MADE AGAINST YOU. HE THEN PAUSED BRIEFLY AS IF TO COLLECT HIMSELF.

WHAT HE SAID NEXT SURPRISED RHEA BECAUSE HE BECAME SLIGHTLY EMOTIONAL, AND SHE COULD FEEL HIS DISCOMFORT. HE TOLD HER THAT AFTER RICO TALKED ABOUT HER NEGATIVELY TO THE KARMIC, LATER THAT NIGHT WHEN HE AND THE TRIBE HAD GONE OUT FOR DRINKS, HE SECRETLY CRIED ABOUT WHAT HE'D SAID ABOUT HER BECAUSE IT HURT HIM TO THE CORE. BUT, HE KNEW HE HAD TO CONTINUE PLAYING HIS PART. HEARING THIS NOW HAD RHEA FIGHTING BACK HER OWN TEARS. RHEA FELT AS IF YEARS OF STRESS AND BURDENS HAD BEEN LIFTED FROM HER AT THAT MOMENT. SHE WHISPERED A PRAYER OF THANKSGIVING AS SOON AS THE CONVERSATION ENDED AND SHE THANKED RICO'S FRIEND. SHE LEFT BROADLAND PARK THAT DAY WITH A LIGHTER HEART AND FEELING

GREATFUL FOR THE KNOWLEDGE AND INFORMATION THAT RICO'S FRIEND HAD GIVEN HER FINALLY LAYING THE NASTY RUMORS TO REST.

RHEA BREATHED A DEEP HEAVY SIGH OF RELIEF FINALLY FEELING THAT ALL THE NEGATIVE TALK AND ACTIONS WERE JUST AN ACT AND THAT RICO WAS REALLY OKAY AFTER ALL.

CHAPTER 36

THE EMPEROR

On the outskirts of town surrounded by a deep wooded area that nearly covered an entire mini mansion, lived several women who called themselves "the Emperor's Family." The ladies were of various ages, backgrounds, ethnicities, skin tones and overall physical appearances.

The house was beautiful and very well maintained by the women who according to the Emperor, must conduct themselves as, "Sister Wives" at all times. So, the women conducted themselves as

FAMILY AT ALL TIMES IN FEAR OF THE EMPEROR'S WRATH IF THEY DIDN'T. ALL HAD WITNESSED HIS WRATH BEFORE, AND NO ONE HAD EVER WANTED TO BE ANYWHERE NEAR IT IF IT WERE TO SHOW UP AGAIN.

THE HOME WAS VERY MODERN AND EQUIPPED WITH SEVERAL AMENITIES FOR THE LADIES AND FOR THE FEW CHILDREN WHO ALSO RESIDED THERE. A CUSTOM POOL, JACUZZI, SAUNA, AND PLAYGROUND WERE ALL PART OF THE MANY DELIGHTS THAT WERE PROVIDED BY THE EMPEROR. THE LADIES WERE VERY EXCITED THAT THE EMPEROR WAS THERE TO SEE THEM TODAY DURING ONE OF HIS ROUTINE VISITS. HIS USUAL CHECK-INS WERE BY SKYPE OR ZOOM AND ON RARE OCCASIONS HE WOULD HAVE DINNER WITH THE FAMILY OR TAKE THE CHILDREN ON AN OUTING. NONE OF THE WOMEN KNEW WHICH OF THE CHILDREN WERE FATHERED BY HIM EXCEPT THE WOMEN THEMSELVES BUT, THEY WERE SWORN TO SECRECY

AND WOULDN'T DARE DISCLOSE THE INFORMATION WITHOUT HIS APPROVAL.

THE EMPEROR ADDRESSED THE LADIES AS A GROUP TODAY TO CHECK ON THE PROGRESS OF HIS INSTRUCTIONS. THERE WERE NINE WOMEN IN ALL WHO HAD BEEN INSTRUCTED BY THE EMPEROR TO MAKE THIS JOB A RED LIGHT PRIORITY. THEY WERE PRESSURED DAILY TO COMPLETE THEIR SISTER CIRCLE BY BAGGING THE EMPRESS. THEY WERE TOLD THAT THIS PARTICULAR WOMAN MUST BE WON AT ALL COSTS. HE SET A BUDGET FOR THE WOMEN TO VISIT THE HIGH PRIESTESS WHO INSTRUCTED THEM ON HOW TO DO MIRROR MAGIC, PICTURE MAGIC SPELLS, AND ANY OTHER SPELLWORK THAT WOULD HELP THEM TO ACHIEVE THIS GOAL SUCCESSFULLY.

THE WOMEN WORKED DILIGENTLY EVERYDAY TO BLOCK THE WOMAN'S HEALTH, FINANCES, CAREER, CREATIVITY, AND LOVE LIFE. THE EMPEROR WAS ADAMANT ABOUT HER

LOVE LIFE BEING BLOCKED BECAUSE HE DIDN'T WANT ANY OTHER MALE SUITORS TO HAVE THE SLIGHTEST CHANCE WITH HER. THE OLDEST SISTER WONDERED WHY THE EMPEROR WAS SO ENAMORED WITH THIS WOMAN AND ON SEVERAL OCCASIONS SHE'D EVEN QUESTIONED HOW A WEALTHY STRONG EMPEROR HAD FALLEN INTO SUCH AN OBSESSION WITH A WOMAN AND WOULD STOP AT NOTHING TO GET HER.

THE EMPEROR TOLD ALL OF THE SISTERS THAT THE EMPRESS WAS THE ONE WOMAN TO COMPLETE THEIR FAMILY AND MAKE IT WHOLE. HE INSTRUCTED THEM TO GET AS MUCH INFORMATION ON THE EMPRESS AS POSSIBLE, AND THAT THEY MUST FOLLOW HER, AND TRACK HER WHEREABOUTS AT ALL TIMES TO REPORT THE INFORMATION DIRECTLY TO HIM. HE TOLD THE WOMEN THAT THEY WOULD BE REWARDED WELL FOR THEIR EFFORTS.

THEY WERE INFORMED THAT THE SISTER WHO FINALLY "BAGGED THE EMPRESS," WOULD RECEIVE WHAT HE CALLED "THE PRESIDENTIAL TREATMENT." THIS CONSISTED OF WINING AND DINING AT THEIR FAVORITE RESTAURANT WITH HIM ON A DATE FOR TWO. THE SISTER WOULD ALSO RECEIVE A FULL SPA TREATMENT, NO CHORES FOR A WEEK, AND THE FINAL PERK WOULD BE A ROMANTIC NIGHT SPENT WITH HIM. HOWEVER, THE WOMEN WERE ADVISED THAT THEY WERE NOT TO COMPETE AGAINST EACH OTHER FOR THE WIN, BUT INSTEAD TO WORK IN UNISON BECAUSE HE WOULD NOT TOLERATE ANY DRAMA OR ANGST AMONG THEM BECAUSE THEIR FAMILY MUST ALWAYS REMAIN DRAMA FREE.

THIS PIQUED THE INTEREST OF ALL OF THE SISTER WIVES AND ALL WANTED TO FIND AS MUCH INFORMATION ON THE WOMAN HE CALLED THE EMPRESS AS THEY COULD TO SATISFY THEIR OWN CURIOSITY SURROUNDING HIS OBSESSION WITH HER. THEY

WONDERED HOW SHE BECAME AN EMPRESS AND HOW THEY TOO COULD BECOME ONE? WHAT WAS SO SPECIAL ABOUT HER BECAUSE ACCORDING TO HER PICTURES AND HER IN PERSON APPEARANCES, SHE WASN'T DROP DEAD GORGEOUS LIKE A MODEL OR A MOVIE STAR?

SHE WAS A LOVELY WOMAN WITH BEAUTIFUL SKIN WHO DRESSED WELL AND SEEMED ALWAYS WELL PUT TOGETHER WITH A UNIQUE STYLE AND A CLOSET THEY ENVIED. AFTER STUDYING HER SOCIAL MEDIA PICS, A FEW OF THE WOMEN TRIED TO MIMIC HER STYLE. A COUPLE OF THE WOMEN TRIED SO HARD TO MIMIC HER, THEY LOOKED LIKE HER DOPPELGANGER. THIS SEEMED TO PLEASE THE EMPEROR, WHICH GOT THEM A COUPLE OF QUICKIES WITH HIM. THE WOMEN WOULD TRY ANYTHING THEY COULD TO HAVE THE EMPEROR SEX THEM UP EVEN IF IT WAS ONLY A QUICKIE. THE EMPEROR HOWEVER DID TRY TO SPEND A LITTLE TIME WITH EACH OF THE LADIES ON

A MONTHLY BASIS TO ALLOW THEM ACCESS TO SOME MUCH APPRECIATED VITAMIN D.

THE EMPEROR, BEING VERY CONTROLLING, TOOK CHARGE OF THE WOMEN'S TIME, SCHEDULE, DIET, FUNDS, AND EVEN THEIR CHOICE OF HAIRSTYLES AND SCENT. HE VIEWED IT AS BEING IN CONTROL OF HIS EMPIRE, BUT TRUTHFULLY, HE WAS WHAT WOULD BE CONSIDERED AS A MODERN-DAY PIMP WITH A STABLE TO SOME. THIS WAS THE LIFESTYLE HE HAD SECRETLY BUILT FOR HIMSELF, AND HE WOULD NOT ALLOW ANYONE TO THREATEN ITS EXISTENCE. THIS WOULD ALLOW HIM TO BECOME HER EMPEROR AND COMPLETE HIS FAMILY.

NO ONE IN SOCIETY SUSPECTED HIM OF LIVING THIS LIFESTYLE AND ALTHOUGH A FEW RUMORS HAD CIRCULATED THROUGHOUT MAHOGANY VALLEY ABOUT SOMEONE REFERRED TO AS THE EMPEROR, NO ONE HAD EVER MET OR SEEN HIM ANYWHERE SO AS FAR AS HE WAS CONCERNED

THEY WERE RUMORS UNTIL PROVEN TO BE REAL. THEY TALKED ABOUT A WEALTHY BUSINESSMAN WHO WENT BY THE NAME AND WHO OWNED A FEW STRIP CLUBS AND OTHER SMALL BUSINESSES AROUND TOWN WHO PREFERRED TO BE KEPT ANONYMOUS. BUT, NO ONE EVER CLAIMED TO HAVE ACTUALLY MET HIM OR KNEW HIS TRUE IDENTITY AND HE PREFERRED TO KEEP IT THAT WAY.

CHAPTER 37

SWEETEST DAY EVENT

ON THE WAY HOME THE WORDS SHARED BETWEEN RHEA AND RICO'S FRIEND RESONATED IN HER MIND LIKE A FAVORITE RECORD ON REPEAT. HER SUPER- POWER INTUITION TOLD HER THAT WHAT HE HAD SHARED WITH HER REGARDING SHE AND RICO'S RELATIONSHIP WAS INDEED THE TRUTH BECAUSE HIS DETAILS WERE DEFINITELY ON POINT.

THAT NIGHT SHE PLAYED SOME OF THE OLD MUSIC THAT SHE AND RICO USED TO LISTEN TO JUST TO SEE WHAT SHE FELT IN HER HEART AFTER HEARING THE INFORMATION AS TO WHY RICO HAD TREATED HER

SO POORLY. THE PROBLEM FOR HER HAD ALWAYS BEEN DIFFICULTY IN FORGIVING PEOPLE AND THAT'S THE ONE AND ONLY FLAW SHE BATTLED WITH IN HER SPIRITUAL LIFE. BUT GOD BEING THE LOVING, GRACEFUL, MERCIFUL, AND FORGIVING FATHER HE WAS, HAD ALWAYS SHOWN PATIENCE WHILE SHE ALLOWED HER HEART TO FORGIVE THOSE WHO WRONGED HER NO MATTER HOW LONG IT TOOK HER.

ON HER KNEES PRAYING THAT NIGHT, SHE ASKED THE DIVINE TO HELP HER ALLOW HER HEART TO OPEN WIDE ENOUGH TO FORGIVE BECAUSE SHE HAD EMOTIONALLY CUT HERSELF OFF TO LOVE AND SHE DOUBTED THAT SHE WOULD EVER ALLOW HER HEART TO FALL IN LOVE WITH ANYONE AGAIN AFTER WHAT RICO HAD PUT HER THROUGH. BUT THAT WAS A DECISION FOR THE FUTURE SHOULD THERE EVER COME AN OPPORTUNITY WORTH INVESTIGATING.

ONE MORNING RHEA SLEPT IN UNTIL LATE AFTERNOON. SHE WAS

IN MUCH NEED OF REST THAT SHE HADN'T BEEN GETTING SINCE ALL THE CHAOS HAD BEGUN. AS SUMMER TURNED INTO FALL, AND AUGUST BECAME SEPTEMBER, THE TOWN OF MAHOGANY VALLEY BECAME DRESSED IN BEAUTIFUL VIBRANT, FALL COLORS.

THERE WAS A BITE IN THE AIR WHICH MADE EARLY MORNINGS AND LATE EVENINGS CRISP WITH THE PROMISE OF WINTER SOON TO ARRIVE. RHEA FOUGHT FEELINGS OF NOSTALGIA REGARDING THE ANNIVERSARY OF THE RELATIONSHIP BETWEEN SHE AND RICO WHICH THEY HAD CELEBRATED IN SEPTEMBER FOR YEARS NOW.

SHE HADN'T HEARD FROM RICO AFTER HER MEETING WITH HIS FRIEND WHICH HAD HER BELIEVING THAT HE KNEW SHE NEEDED SPACE TO PROCESS ALL THE NEWS SHE HAD RECEIVED. BUT FOR RHEA, HER HEALING WAS PRIORITY AND SELF-LOVE WAS AT THE CENTER OF HER HEALING PROCESS.

SHE THOUGHT ABOUT THEIR RELATIONSHIP AND WONDERED HOW SOMETHING SO POWERFUL AND MAGICAL WAS ABLE TO GO SO WRONG AND TOTALLY CRUMBLE TO THE GROUND AS IF IT HAD NEVER EVEN EXISTED. SHE THOUGHT ABOUT HOW HE ALLOWED HIMSELF TO BECOME SO TOXIC AND BEHAVED AS A SERIAL CHEATER WHO CONNECTED WITH A DARK ENTITY WHO ONLY BROUGHT HIM GRIEF.

WAS HE REALLY MISSING HER, OR WAS HE JUST HAVING COOKIE WITHDRAWS FROM ALL THE SEX THAT WAS INCREDIBLE BETWEEN THEM? YES, SHE ADMITTED THAT SHE MISSED THE PHYSICAL COMPONANT OF THEIR RELATIONSHIP. BUT, NO MATTER HOW SHE MISSED THE RELATIONSHIP WHEN IT WAS HEALTHY, SHE WOULD NOT EVER ALLOW HERSELF TO PLAY ON ANYONE'S PLAYGROUND AGAIN WITHOUT HER PERMISSION.

RHEA COMPLETED SOME OF THE PROJECTS SHE'D BEEN WORKING ON

AND ALLOWED HERSELF TO TAKE A MUCH-NEEDED BREAK. AS SEPTEMBER TURNED INTO OCTOBER, THE TOWN OF MAHOGANY VALLEY WAS ALIVE WITH PLANNED SOCIAL EVENTS FOR THE SEASON. ALTHOUGH THERE WERE SEVERAL EVENTS PLANNED FOR THE UPCOMING WEEKEND, THE ONE THAT MOST PEOPLE IN RHEA'S SOCIAL CIRCLE WOULD BE ATTENDING WOULD BE A THEMED DINNER DANCE.

THE SOCIAL GROUP THAT HAD BEEN HOSTING A VERY NICE, SWEETEST DAY DINNER DANCE EVERY YEAR WERE CALLED THE ELEGANT GEMS. THE GEMS HAD BEEN CREATED AND MANAGED BY HER COUSIN LENA BARKLEY. IN RHEA'S OPINION, THIS WAS THE ONE THAT WAS CONSIDERED BY FAR THE CHOICE FOR CLASS AND ELEGANCE. RHEA WOULD BE ATTENDING THE EVENT SOLO THAT NIGHT, SO SHE FUSSED AND FRETTED OVER HER OUTFIT WHICH WAS THEMED IN THE ERA OF THE ROARING TWENTIES.

THERE WERE SEVERAL OTHER EVENTS HAPPENING IN THE TOWN THAT WEEKEND AROUND DIFFERENT SOCIAL CIRCLES AND ESPECIALLY IN THE BLACK COMMUNITY. "BLACK-TIVITY" (BLACK ACTIVITY) WAS IN THE AIR AND SEVERAL COUPLES MADE THEIR PLANS TO ATTEND ONE OR MORE OF WHAT THE SOCIAL CALENDAR HAD TO OFFER.

AS USUAL, THE GEMS HAD GONE ALL OUT TO MAKE THE EVENT ENJOYABLE FOR ALL ITS ATTENDEES AND EVERYONE WHO HAD ATTENDED THEIR EVENTS IN THE PAST KNEW THEY WOULDN'T BE DISAPPOINTED. THEY WERE KNOWN FOR HOSTING AN EVENT FILLED WITH GREAT ENTERTAINMENT, GOOD FOOD, MUSIC AND RAFFLES. RHEA FELT THIS COULD NOT HAVE COME AT A BETTER TIME BECAUSE SHE MOST CERTAINLY NEEDED THIS EVENING TO BE A WELCOME DISTRACTION FROM WORK AND OTHER STRESSFUL DAILY ISSUES.

RHEA TOOK ONE LAST LOOK IN THE MIRROR AND ADJUSTED HER FEATHERED FLAPPER'S HEADBAND BEFORE EXITING HER HOME. SHE HAD TO ADMIT THAT SHE WAS FULL OF ANTICIPATION REGARDING ENDLESS POSSIBILITIES FOR THE NIGHT WHICH ALLOWED HER TO KEEP AN OPEN MIND ABOUT THE NIGHTS' FESTIVITIES. THE PARKING AREA WAS SLIGHTLY FULL WHICH TOLD RHEA THAT THE EVENT WAS ALREADY STARTING, AND SHE WAS RIGHT ON TIME.

AS PREVIOUSLY PREDICTED, THE EVENT PRESENTED ITSELF WELL. THE DÉCOR WAS UPSCALE, AND EVERYONE DRESSED IN THEIR ROARING TWENTIES THEMED GEAR LOOKED AMAZING. THE PARTY WAS OFF TO A GREAT START AND RHEA LOOKED FOR CANDY, NOVA, AND THE REST OF HER FRIENDS. THEY ALL ARRIVED AROUND THE SAME TIME AND FOUND GREAT TABLES NEAR THE FRONT. RHEA SPOKE BRIEFLY TO HER COUSIN LENA AND CONGRATULATED HER ON ANOTHER SUCCESSFUL

EVENT. THEY SPOKE BRIEFLY, THEN WENT TOWARDS THEIR TABLES.

RHEA RECONNECTED WITH SEVERAL SCHOOL MATES WHOM SHE HADN'T SEEN IN SEVERAL YEARS. EVERYONE SEEMED TO BE HAVING A GREAT TIME AS THE MUSIC, DRINKS AND GOOD FOOD FLOWED NON-STOP FOR THE ATTENDEE'S ENJOYMENT. LIVE ENTERTAINMENT HAD EVERYONE'S ATTENTION AND RHEA WAS GRATEFUL THAT SHE DECIDED TO TAKE A CHANCE AND ATTEND THE EVENT.

AFTER DINNER, RHEA DECIDED TO GO OUTSIDE AND GET SOME MUCH-NEEDED AIR. AS SHE STOOD OUTSIDE CONTEMPLATING WHETHER TO GO TOWARDS HER VEHICLE, SHE FELT A LIGHT TAP ON HER SHOULDER FROM BEHIND. RHEA HESITATED TO TURN BECAUSE INTUITIVELY SHE COULD FEEL HIS PRESENCE EVEN BEFORE HE APPROACHED. BEFORE SHE COULD TURN TO ADDRESS HIS INTRUSION, HE TOOK BOTH OF HER SHOULDERS AND TURNED HER AROUND TO FACE HIM.

As Rico took Rhea by her shoulders turning her in his direction to face him, he very gently pulled her body into his. He then embraced her head and planted a kiss on the top as he held her close to his chest. Rhea did not fight or pull away but allowed him to continue to hold her face and head close to his chest. Rico held her close enough so that she could feel and hear his racing heartbeat. She remembered how they held each other during lovemaking and how both of their heartbeats became in synch every time. Rico was hesitant to let Rhea go and for Rhea, all time stood still like it did at the club where she felt they were moving in slow motion underwater. So engrossed in each other's embrace, neither Twin heard anyone approaching until words were spoken.

Johnnie Harris had approached the scene without their

KNOWLEDGE AND WAS LOOKING VERY ANGRY AT WHAT HE WAS WITNESSING. RHEA, COMING BACK TO HERSELF TRIED TAKING A STEP BACK FROM RICO BUT HE WAS RELUCTANT TO LET HER GO FULLY. HE DID HOWEVER LET ONE ARM CONTINUE TO WRAP ITSELF AROUND HER SHOULDERS. RHEA SUSPECTED RICO WAS ONLY DOING THIS TO AGGRAVATE JOHNNIE FURTHER IN RETALIATION OF THEIR LAST ENCOUNTER. RICO CLEARLY WANTED TO MAKE A STATEMENT AND PUSH JOHNNIE'S BUTTONS.

FEELING THE TENSION GROWING BETWEEN THE TWO VERY HANDSOME AND TALENTED MEN, RHEA KNEW SHE NEEDED TO MAKE SOME KIND OF GESTURE TO DE-ESCALATE THEIR RISING TEMPERS BEFORE IT WAS TOO LATE. ONCE AGAIN, SHE TRIED TO PULL AWAY FROM RICO WHILE GREETING JOHNNIE WITH A QUICK HELLO AND A NICE SMILE. HOWEVER, RICO BEING IN THE MIND-SET THAT HE'D FINALLY GOTTEN A CHANCE TO GET HER CLOSE TO HIM AGAIN AFTER

ALL THE TIME THAT HAD PASSED, HE WASN'T ABOUT TO MISS THIS OPPORTUNITY.

BEING SO CAUGHT UP IN THE MOMENT, NEITHER OF THE THREE SAW A CROWD GATHERING AROUND THEM TO SEE HOW THIS WOULD ALL PLAY ITSELF OUT. BECAUSE OF THEIR LOCAL CELEBRITY STATUS HERE IN THE MAHOGANY VALLEY AND ABROAD, BOTH JOHNNIE AND RICO WERE ALWAYS OF INTEREST TO PEOPLE AND ANYTHING SURROUNDING THEM WOULD BE CONSIDERED NEWSWORTHY. MOST EVERYONE IN THE LOCAL ENTERTAINMENT INDUSTRY FELT THAT THERE HAD ALWAYS BEEN A SLIGHT UNSPOKEN RIVALRY BETWEEN THE TWO, BUT BOTH WOULD HAVE DENIED IT IF ASKED.

JOHNNIE SPOKE DIRECTLY TO RICO THIS TIME SAYING, "LET HER GO RICO." RICO TOLD JOHNNIE TO MIND HIS OWN DAMNED BUSINESS AND STAY OUT OF HIS. JOHNNIE IGNORED HIS WARNING AND REPEATED "LET HER

GO MAN." RHEA BECOMING MORE NERVOUS BY THE SECOND REPEATED JOHNNIE'S WORDS ASKING RICO TO LET GO BUT HE WASN'T HAVING IT AND POLITELY TOLD HER NO WHILE STILL MAINTAINING HIS GRIP ON HER.

THE CROWD SEEMED TO GROW LARGER BY THE MINUTE AND WHISPERING VOICES COULD BE HEARD IN ITS MIX, BUT THE TWO MEN SEEMED OBLIVIOUS TO ANYTHING OTHER THAN THEIR POSITION AND NEITHER SEEMED WILLING TO BACK DOWN AND WALK AWAY THIS TIME.

FINALLY, JOHNNIE SPOKE, BUT THIS TIME HIS WORDS WERE AIMED DIRECTLY TOWARDS RHEA AND WERE SIMPLY "MAKE A CHOICE." SURPRISED AT HIS WORDS AND QUITE LITERALLY CAUGHT OFF GUARD RHEA RESPONDED, "WHAT?" AGAIN, JOHNNIE REPEATED HIS WORDS TELLING HER TO "MAKE A CHOICE RIGHT NOW" BUT THIS TIME HE SAID IT LOUDER AND ADDED, "THIS WILL BE RESOLVED RIGHT HERE, TONIGHT, RHEA."

RICO CHOSE THAT MOMENT TO SPEAK UP AND REPEATED JOHNNIE'S WORDS SAYING, "I AGREE, THE TIME HAS COME MY LOVE." RHEA LOOKED AT BOTH MEN WHOM SHE HAD LOVED AND ADORED FOR SO LONG AS THE CROWD'S WHISPERS BECAME LOUDER, AND THE TENSION GREW INTO ANTICIPATION. EVERYONE WAS EAGERLY AWAITING HER RESPONSE. ALL EYES WERE DIRECTED TOWARDS HER AND BOTH MEN HAD TAKEN A FIRM STANCE IMPATIENTLY AWAITING THE ANSWER THAT WOULD AFFECT BOTH EITHER NEGATIVELY OR POSITIVELY. RHEA TOOK A DEEP BREATH AS SHE FOUGHT BACK THE TEARS THAT HAD BEGUN TO ROLL DOWN HER FACE WITHOUT WARNING.

AGAIN, SHE LOOKED AT BOTH MEN, SO HANDSOME AND STRONG. MEN THAT MOST WOMEN WOULD GIVE UP THEIR SINGLEHOOD FOR IN A HEARTBEAT. SHE CONSIDERED THEM BOTH A BLESSING, AND SHE WAS FOREVER GRATEFUL FOR THE EXPERIENCES THEIR RELATIONSHIPS HAD BROUGHT

TO HER LIFE GOOD AND BAD. SHE HAD LOVED THEM AND RESPECTED THEM THROUGH THE GOOD AND BAD TIMES. NOW, SHE HAD A DECISION TO MAKE WHICH WOULD TAKE HER TO THE NEXT LEVEL OF HER LIFE'S PATH.

RHEA DID THE ONLY THING SHE COULD AT THAT MOMENT. SHE LOOKED IN ANOTHER DIRECTION. THE ONLY DIRECTION WHERE SHE COULD GET THE ANSWER SHE NEEDED. HER ONLY SOURCE OF EVERYTHING THAT HAD GUIDED HER LIFE UNTIL THIS VERY MOMENT. SHE LOOKED TOWARDS THE HEAVENS AND WHISPERED A SILENT PRAYER TO GOD. "PLEASE SHOW ME THE WAY FATHER, I NEED YOU DESPERATELY RIGHT NOW."

THE END

DIVINELY GUIDED

September was the time
You gave yourself and I gave mine.
We came together to fill a passion,
Never knowing this would be a blessing.

We both agreed that we would try it,
Neither knew this was divinely guided.
Soon reality brought obstacles our way,
But the angels said, "Oh no, this love is here to stay."
That's when passion turned into true love,
A love that must be sent down from above
This love is divinely, divinely guided.
We can't stop true love,
Only the angels can from above.

This love is divinely, divinely
guided.
No one can part it,
  it was heavenly started,
And sent down to us from above.
He held up his mirror and he
saw me,
I held up my mirror and the
reflection was he this love, true
love is so very rare,
Nothing can stop it when God
makes a pair.

When we make sweet love,
The angels sing up above
Saying
2 heart beats become one,
Beating loudly as a drum,
2 spirits, one soul,
Under heaven's control.
This love is divinely, so divinely
guided,
No, no, you can't stop true love,
Only the angels can from above.
No one can part it,
It was heavenly started
And sent down to us from above.

THIS LOVE IS DIVINELY, DIVINELY
GUIDED, YES, IT IS,
OH NO YOU CAN'T STOP TRUE LOVE,
 ONLY THE ANGELS CAN FROM ABOVE.
NO ONE CAN PART IT,
IT WAS HEAVENLY STARTED
AND SENT DOWN TO US FROM ABOVE
WRITTEN   BY   ROSE
WATSON-RICHARDSON
8/2021

www.ingramcontent.com/pod-product-compliance
Lightning Source LLC
Chambersburg PA
CBHW071229210726
48293CB00002B/630